'WE'LL NEVER KNOW'

by Matthew Tree

Based on a true story

Published by: England-Is-A-Bitch Productions
•
Book design by vagabond
Instagram @vgbnd
Twitter @vgbnd

ISBN: 9798873533862

PART ONE

I

I didn't have much to do with my father and he never had much to do with me, partly because (after a stint as an undergraduate at Lancaster University), I decided to knuckle down to the rest of my studies on the far side of the Atlantic – the biggest ocean I could find – and partly because during the last years of his not-overlong life he was a feckless, albeit functioning, drunk. During that period I went to see him just a couple of times at his last bolt-hole, a Riviera village so small it couldn't boast so much as a Mayor, and I didn't stay long, for either visit. To see this man who was crawling towards his sixtieth birthday and doing nothing but hanging about with a small bunch of locals, talking about cars and the weather as they worked their way through a merry-go-round of beers, wines and spirits in one or t'other of the village's two bars, was not something that was about to stir up whatever embers of filial love that might still have retained a little warmth; to add disdain to disappointment, in his pre-alcoholic life he'd made his living by teaching watercolour techniques at a variety of council-funded evening classes in London, until his own father passed away and left him a house in Pinner whose sale kept him in enough clover from then on to quietly sweep whatever creative itching he'd ever felt under his mental carpet and dedicate himself to what amounted to biding his time until the Reaper ran him to earth at age fifty-nine. In 2045.

I felt sorry, for him, my Dad, in the same way I feel sorry for writers who nobody's ever heard of, for musicians with one-hit wonders that no one can remember, or for actors who never make it out of the supporting cast, or even for clowns who've spent their working lives at children's parties. Dear God, I would think, when waking up some mornings, what must have it been like for *him*, opening his eyes every single morning to face the daylight with a hangover kicking him in the head, knowing that he'd bet his life, time and again, on low cards and losing numbers; that time and again he'd seen the chips swept away from him until there was nothing under his eyes except worn baize? Sisyphus, eat your fucking heart out.

And it was because I felt sorry for him that from an early age I knew that whatever I did with my life, it would have to be done in a way that was the precise opposite of my father's. I didn't want anyone, anywhere, to be pitying me. Instead of the lack of self-confidence that ended up blighting his life, I would be proud of myself, no matter what; instead of his irresoluteness, I would have ambition; instead of cultivating futile aspirations – he had wasted his unpaid time making oil paintings that were no good and never would be – I'd choose something I knew I was good at or could make myself good at. In short, I would make his feebleness the foil to my future, until he'd become little more to me, in my imagination, than an unvisited gravestone. I didn't hate him, even though it'd have been easier if I had; I just felt it was a shame that *he'd* been my father. After all, like anyone else, I could have done with some paternal guidance, but instead of that I had to steer my way around him, keeping my distance lest any of his pusillanimity should rub off on me.

I studied myself sick in the States, going from master's degree to master's degree until I had a thorough command of the formal, social and natural sciences – from systems theory to Earth science, from astronomy to anthropology; and of on-going developments in all these fields, as well as the history of science itself. But I never planned on a career as a professional scientist, because the peeks I'd had into the scientific world put me off right from the start: it was a world, so it seemed to me, full of people who were more competitive than athletes, each trying to out-research the other, often working for donkeys' years on identical or similar projects; then, when a rival pipped them to the post, some of them would lapse into clinical depression or, on occasion, even top themselves.

My path lay elsewhere, and I'd already mapped it out: I'd barely turned thirty when I went back home and became the chief science correspondent of one of England's most respected broadsheets. I gained a reputation as someone who could explain the most complicated scientific phenomena in a way that every layman and laid woman could understand. Which is why, alongside my regular columns, my paper decided to open up a weekly Q&A section for readers with pertinent questions which I answered, shooting straight from the hip with clear, accurate and well-written replies. Which is probably also why the two popular science books I wrote over that same period sold in reassuringly satisfactory quantities. In short, when my thirty-fifth birthday rolled around, I'd become one of the go-to experts on matters empirical.

By which time, in my head, my late father was deader than ever.

II

At the paper, I had my own king-sized, screened-off work station. I could have worked perfectly well from home, but home wasn't for working in. Home was a three-room flat in South Kensington, a stone's throw from the V&A. Home was a wall-mounted 88-inch television screen, a floor-standing single speaker, a double bed, a small, shiny kitchen, a couple of armchairs, a coffee table, parquet flooring and a view of a square. Home was for eating, watching TV, reading and sending and receiving messages on a tablet. As for sex, I preferred to take the temporary work-experience students who passed through the editorial office on their six-month tours of duty to medium-priced hotels, because I didn't want them sniffing around my work-free home.

They – or at least the pretty ones – were more than enough to satisfy my needs and their fleetingness meant that I could steer well clear of anything resembling a relationship.

(That was something else that my father had allowed to fuck him up: after being dumped gently by Mum he fell into the arms of a younger woman who a few months later died prematurely in Belarus, in circumstances I've never been able to clarify and which he refused to talk about. He never got over losing Mum and afterwards he never got over losing this other woman, so for quite a while he was pining for both of them simultaneously, which must have been a humungous bummer, and yet there was no one to blame for it except himself: if he hadn't allowed himself to wallow in sentiments that no longer had any point to them, he would have been a happier, more personable man, instead of the misery-guts he apparently preferred to be.)

I would sit myself down at my work station at ten, go out for a sandwich at twelve, get back at half past and work until four. Five days a week.

From time to time, I had to go to – or was invited to – various scientific congresses and conferences around the world, to make sure I heard about the latest discoveries from the horses' mouths.

As scientific events do not happen on a daily basis, the writing of my informative articles took up little more than one afternoon per week. But for the Q&A section I received dozens of emails, asking me about everything under and beyond the sun. I had to wade through all these queries and fish out one or preferably two to which the weekly answer would make good copy. First I weeded out the jokers ('Do flatulent surgeons contaminate the operating theatre?') followed by the nutters ('What is the exact location of Atlantis?'); I would also have to eliminate the science students and on occasion bona fide scientists whose enquiries tended to be too recherché for a general readership ('What is a likely source for deep-space neutrinos?'); only then did I finally get around to the ones that would interest a wide range of readers ('How long is Earth going to exist?').

I'd sit there in my Timberlands, my jeans and my button-down shirt, loving the regularity of the routine, loving the knowledge that I was making good money with each tap of the keys, loving the praises that more often than not were embedded in the emailed questions I received, loving having a by-line in a big newspaper, which was a fine form of fame, making me well-known without turning me into a clown or a ham, like, say, so many TV celebrities. Like all of them, in fact.

Back then I revelled in my ability to take no shit from a soul; and also in the sexism I wore on my sleeve (partly because I'd discovered that it turned some women on) and in my forthrightness, which made it possible for me to give orders – or make requests – in a way that ensured they were never ignored. I knew there were people who thought I was far too full of myself, who despised my macho mind-set, who might even, indeed, have considered me to be a pompous, self-important bastard, but I didn't give a damn and was proud of not giving it. My life was a one-way street with just me walking its length, and I wasn't about to let anyone or anything pull me in any wrong directions. And if my mind was ever disturbed by any self-doubt about my self-confidence, I would flick such qualms into the wastebasket with the conviction that I simply was the way I was and there was nothing I could do about it even if I wanted to. Which I didn't. Not back then.

From time to time, my work address being available on the paper's website, I got requests for a personal meeting from women who invariably attached a photo. Attractive as they sometimes tended to be, I would always politely decline, not wanting to run any risks: you never could tell if they were who they said they were; or if they had become infatuated, or were ill in the head.

Then, one day, I got a request for a personal meeting from a woman who wasn't trying to seduce me. And she didn't attach a photo, either.

III

'Dear Mr Wyndham, I am writing to you concerning a matter of the greatest importance, convinced that you will be able to help. It concerns my husband. I really don't want to go into any details in an email. For that reason, It would be better if we met personally. Please let me know when and where would be convenient for you. Kind regards, Melissa Hogg.'

I found this downright impertinent. She wasn't *asking* me, she was as good as *telling* me to meet up with her, even though I didn't know her from Eve. I deleted the message and got on with my work. Just before I left the office she sent me another mail.

'Please don't give me the brush-off, Mr Wyndham; I promise you, this is not a crank message. My husband has been involved in matters scientific, and that is why I – and he – believe you may be able to help. More than that I really cannot say except in a private conversation. Please be so kind as to accept my request for an appointment. Yours, Melissa Hogg.'

This second message – both, I now noticed, had been sent from a mobile phone – had a note of desperation in it that rubbed me up the wrong way. Besides, if this was to do with her husband, why didn't he contact me himself? I decided to brush this female pest off.

'Dear Ms Hogg, I am sorry to inform you that you are writing to the wrong person. It sounds as if your husband is in some kind of trouble, but I am not a policeman. However, as you are surely aware, there are plenty of people who are. I suggest that you get in touch with them.'

And with that, I picked up the small rucksack containing a couple of peer-reviewed journals and the latest issue of *New Scientist*, and headed for the exit, pausing only to chat for a moment with a new intern, a truly gorgeous-looking red-head who had made it quite clear that she didn't object to my ostensibly solicitous enquiries about how she was fitting in. As I took the lift, I felt pretty sure I could offer to take her out for dinner sometime towards the end of the week and get yes for an answer.

The paper was located not far from the Tate Britain, and I had come to enjoy my daily after-work walk along the river and through Victoria Tower Gardens on my way to Westminster tube station. There was something about the water-scented breeze that I found comfortingly Londonish, as if the city were telling me I was in the right place at the right time with the right job: in short, that all was right with my world.

Yet, no sooner had I walked into the gardens, when a woman who had been tapping furiously on her mobile looked up, saw me and stood up from a bench that was to the right of the entrance. She had long, straggly, starting-to-grey hair and one of those concerned, intense faces I've always found off-putting. On top of which, being at least halfway through her forties as I surmised she must have been, she was way too old for me.

"Mr Timothy Wyndham!"

This bloody woman – Melissa Hogg, *sans doute* – was wearing a hippyish cotton dress with a dark brown and blue pattern that might have suited her when she was twenty. She held out a hand. I raised mine.

"How did you know I'd be walking through here at this time of day?"

She put down her hand, disconcerted.

"Your photo appears next to your by-line so I know what you look like. I assumed you might ignore or reject my messages. After all, we don't know each other and you're a busy man. So yesterday I took the liberty of checking what time you left work and which route you took. I'm so sorry, I know that this is highly irreg– "

"It's what the law calls stalking. And if you bother me just once more, I'll let the law know about it."

That made this ridiculous woman flinch.

"I wouldn't have done something so unusual if time wasn't of the essence."

Her face, more intense than ever. The gall of this middle-aged bag! I confess, however, that her talk about time being of the essence piqued my curiosity. But not enough.

"I'm not in the dilly-dallying mood, so I'd appreciate it if you would be on your way, and allow me to be on mine."

She gawked at me, mouth casting about for words, clearly not about to give up. Maybe, I fretted, she was something worse than a pest.

"My husband works for the MoD. A special unit. He's not allowed to talk to the media. He's monitored. Closely. He would like to set up a discreet meeting. Well, clandestine, really."

A nervous half-laugh. She didn't *sound* as if she was making it up.

"If your husband works for the MoD, you need to talk to our Defence and Security Correspondent. I can text you her details, if you wish."

"My husband's work is strictly scientific."

"Is it now? What's his speciality?"

I said, mentally kicking myself for having continued the conversation.

"He's an astrophysicist."

Eh?

"What's an astrophysicist doing working on a defence project?"

"You'd have to talk to him, I'm a bit hazy on the technical details."

Mainly because I wanted to get her out of my hair, and partly because my curiosity had been piqued a little more, I pulled out my wallet and handed her a business card.

"I can't promise anything. But if your husband wants to set up a meeting and I happen to be free, I'll try and make it. Text only, no phone calls."

"Thank-you!"

Said with a bleat to it. I left her standing there and hurried off to what had become the welcoming beacon of Westminster station.

IV

If time was of the essence for that woman, she wasn't in a hurry to show it: the days went by after that Monday meeting without a texted dicky-bird from her or her husband and by the time Friday had rolled around I'd concluded she was one sandwich short of a picnic.

Meanwhile, I was spending incrementally longer periods of time pretending to be solicitous about the red-headed intern's progress, standing by her desk, checking her work, offering advice. (I made sure, as per usual, not to do anything inappropriate, such as gently stroking her shoulder.)

On Friday morning, when things were quiet in the office I ambled over to her desk.

"Everything OK?"

She looked up at me with those large blue pupils of hers.

"Everything."

I winced and hummed and hawed for a few moments, making out I was a bit nervous about what I was about to say, a technique which usually worked wonders. Then I went in for the kill.

"I wonder if I could ask you something which isn't to do with your work?"

Without taking her eyes from her screen nor her fingers from her keyboard, she said:

"Go ahead."

"If you say no, I'll understand completely and promise that I won't repeat the question."

"What question?"

There was a nonchalance in her voice which I found unusual.

"Do you think you could bear to have dinner with me tonight?"

She glanced at me then went back to concentrating on her screen.

"Where would this dinner be?"

I wasn't expecting the question, but I had the answer anyway.

"There's a new Argentinian near Hyde Park which I'd love to try but am loathe to do so on my own."

"Is that because you haven't got a girlfriend?"

Sassy, this kind of banter. I found myself liking it.

"How did you guess?"

"What time?"

Wow.

"Would Marble Arch tube at seven be OK?"

"Only if you're punctual. I don't like to be kept hanging around."

Double wow.

"I'll get there a few minutes earlier, just to make sure."

"You do that."

Face still facing the screen, she fluttered a handful of fingers at me by way of terminating the conversation. As I wandered back to my work station, it occurred to me that I didn't know her name.

*

Adalyn. I'd had to ask her how it was spelt. She was looking at the menu on the far side of a thick oak table, the restaurant's open brick work – on which a row of *maté* gourds were displayed – behind her. Now that I had the time to observe her red hair, it seemed to have some kind of electric gleam to it. Her lips were not too thick and not too thin and not made-up. Her skin was on the pale side, something I'd always found attractive.

Once we had our steaks in front of us, I did my usual trick of asking her what she wanted to do with her life after she'd finished her stint at the paper (taking care to say this in a way that implied I might be able to help). Carefully cutting off a piece of the sirloin she'd ordered almost raw:

"I've already done quite a lot. I'm twenty-seven years old."

Twenty-seven! She looked younger, but the matter-of-fact, no-monkey-business manner in which she'd spoken, left me in no doubt that she was telling the truth.

"That's a little odd. Most of the interns tend to be in their late teens, twenty-one, tops."

She looked at me, chewing the piece of meat, and only after the time it had taken her to do that and swallow it, did she say:

"Do you prefer younger women?"

It was a genuine question, bereft of criticism. I had to think.

"Not necessarily. It depends."

"On what?"

"On who they are, what they're like as people, not what age they are."

I hoped that one would pass.

"So if you met a – for you – ugly fifty-year-old who was an interesting person, you'd try and date her?"

Oh God.

"I don't know. I haven't yet had the pleasure."

Flippancy to the rescue, so I hoped. And thankfully, she changed the subject.

"What got you interested in science?"

The answer to this, I had off pat.

"Because it deals in reality. Everything science does is about investigating or harnessing reality. And in an age when reality is constantly being pushed aside by false information, wishful thinking, or superstition masquerading as knowledge, well, science is a balm, a solace. A place of safety, if you will."

Off pat I might have had it, but I'd never delivered it with such conviction, such seriousness. It was as if I didn't want to let this ever more attractive young woman down.

"And what," she said, having ingested another chunk of meat, "does science do when it comes up against phenomena which might or might not be real?"

"Such as?"

Her eyes on mine, she shrugged, deliciously.

"Oh, say, telepathy."

Had I known she was going to say that?

"ESP, under whose umbrella, as I'm sure you know, telepathy comes, has been investigated exhaustively for over a century and not only is there no evidence for its existence, but there is not even a plausible hypothesis for its existence."

"Uh-huh."

Or at least that's what I thought I heard her say, muffled as her voice was by food.

*

When we'd finished our meal, I suggested she try an Armagnac (which impresses them because they usually don't know what

Armagnac is; and besides, it gets them into the mood). She shook her head.

"I don't like Armagnac. I'll have a Frangelico, if they've got any."

They had, and I found myself feeling relieved, as if the restaurant's not having Frangelico would have reflected badly on me. When our respective liqueurs came I raised my glass and she raised hers. I took a sip from mine and she knocked hers down in one swift go, then put the glass back on the table. I looked at her and she looked back.

"Was it good?"

She gave a non-committal shrug.

"It was OK. It always is."

*

We stepped out of the restaurant fastening up our coats: it was autumn: the evenings were turning cold. She sniffed the air.

"Dead leaves," she said.

"It's autumn," I said.

"Uh-huh."

"I'm guessing you must live in a park-free, leaf-free borough."

We had started to move in the direction I had gently taken.

"I don't live in London."

That surprised me.

"You commute in for an unpaid job? That must be costing you a fortune."

Walking slowly next to me but at a distance that precluded any shoulder rubbing, she kept her eyes on the pavement.

"I like travelling."

She really was different from the others. Different age, different tastes, different answers. That excited me. We were approaching the end of Strathearn Place. Not far to go now. As we turned into Stanhope Terrace, I made my usual play.

"Look, I don't want you to think I'm being forward, but that's exactly what I'm going to be. There's a very comfortable hotel not far from here. I'm sure you know what I'm getting at."

And I gave her my best twilight smile, understanding and cheeky. She finally looked up.

"You wish to sleep with me."

It wasn't a question. *Wish?*

"I do."

She stopped right at the start of the street that led directly to the hotel I had in mind. She touched my arm without taking hold of it, as if checking I was real.

"I have other plans for tonight."

My heart, as they say, sank.

"I wasn't aware you had a boyfriend. I'm sorry."

"I don't, so don't be."

"I'll walk you to the nearest tube."

But before I could set off, she tugged my sleeve, gently, to stop me.

"If you want, I could masturbate you."

Taken aback, I blinked several times.

"I'm sorry?"

"We could go into the park and, if needs be, I could masturbate you."

This was the kind of suggestion I had, on occasion, made to a couple of the others who hadn't wanted to go all the way. And although the suggestion had come, unusually, from her and not me, had she been any of the others I would have said 'Why not?', taken her by the hand – *that* hand – and accompanied her into the bushes. But looking into those calm blue eyes and at her electric red hair, I decided there and then that I would seduce her to the point where she would want to do whatever came to my mind.

"Thanks for the offer," I said, jokingly, "but I think that would be a bit sordid, don't you?"

Without frowning, she said:

"Sordid?"

As if she didn't know what the word meant. I didn't feel like providing a definition.

"Look, you've got somewhere else to be, and I've always got some work to catch up on, so why don't we call it a night? A night which I've very much enjoyed, by the way."

"It was fine," she said, without stressing a single word.

"Maybe we could do dinner again some time."

She nodded:

"I know where the tube station is; no need to accompany me."

With which, she walked off. I hailed a cab, feeling an inexplicably urgent need to get back home as soon as possible, to the three rooms, the TV screen, the shiny kitchen, the view of a square.

*

Before lying down single in my double bed, I checked my mail.

'*Could you please be at the Croydon Park and Ride, tomorrow at 7am? I'm sorry to be so precipitate but, as I think I mentioned to you, time is of the essence. Thank-you. Melissa.*'

'Thank-you'? As if I'd already agreed to be there, the pushy cow. But perhaps, it occurred to me, this might put an end to the whole business, once and for all.

V

It was bloody cold out in Croydon's bloody park and ride. I was standing there like a proper berk, shivering and staring at the sea of cars that surrounded me under a sky the colour of whipped cream. The cafeteria was closed, of course, at that time of morning. Only the occasional stopping of a bus heading for central London provided any sign of human life.

So quiet was it, such a hush reigned over the lacklustre metal roofs and bonnets, that the beep of my cell phone gave me a start. A message from a number I didn't recognise, telling me to walk two rows up and five cars along until I found a Renault Four.

*

It was a beat-up off-white heap that must have slid off the assembly line some sixty years ago. I leaned down to peek through the window, expecting to see that wrinkled hippy again but instead there was a jumpy man at the wheel, signalling with a flapping hand that I step into the front passenger seat.

"Thank-you for coming."

He was wearing a red suit with a tartan pattern on it and a navy-blue shirt. He had a high forehead on the crest of which clumps of dishevelled grey hair bobbed as he leaned across me and closed my door.

"Can't be too careful."

A milky smile. He stuck out a hand.

"Quentin Hogg."

I shook it. He gave an inappropriate giggle.

"I don't really know where to start!"

For fuck's sake.

"How about telling me why you've asked me to this benighted car park at the crack of dawn? Because if you don't, I'm out of here, pronto."

He made rapid calming gestures with his hands that only riled me some more.

"Of course, of course! As my wife told you, I work for the Ministry of Defence."

The car door on my side swung open.

"You have to slam it hard, otherwise it won't close properly."

I slammed it hard. It closed properly.

"Wait a minute. If you're working for the MoD, how come you're driving this old crock?"

"Oh, I paid a friend to buy it for me."

"You haven't answered my question."

"As it's been purchased just for this meeting, I didn't want to spend too much money."

I looked at his apologetic face.

"Just for this meeting?"

"At home I have a somewhat smarter vehicle. A Jaguar actually, but that's neither here nor there."

"But, why –?"

He cut in, agitatedly.

"My other car would have been traced and followed. Nobody knows about this one."

I wondered if he was more seriously ill than his wife. Paranoid, perhaps. Schizophrenic?

"Why would anyone want to follow you?"

"I was getting round to that. What my wife didn't tell you, because she doesn't know very much about it, is the department I've been assigned to."

"And what department would that be?"

"The Office of Special Investigations. OSPI, in the jargon."

"Which does…?"

"We look at artefacts that are difficult to classify."

I had a nasty feeling that I knew where this might be going.

"Could you be a little more specific?"

"My job deals with elements forwarded by a small unit of the Fleet Air Arm, known as Code Orange (which liaises on a regular basis with its American opposite number, by the way) to the DIS and then –"

"DIS?"

"Defence Intelligence Staff. And if the DIS think it's worth it, they pass it on to the outfit I work for. The OSPI."

"And what kind of things do the good people at Defence Intelligence find 'worth it'?"

He looked away, took a deep sigh, and, as if ashamed, said:

"Recovered aerial craft of unknown origin."

I should have bloody guessed.

"You're into UFOs?"

Now he looked at me, his eyes dilated, his lips quivering.

"Well, I suppose you could put it like that. Except they're not completely unidentified."

"What?"

"We have them. Before our eyes. As visible as my hand."

He held up his hand, palm out. My turn to sigh.

"And they're from outer space, I presume."

"We're still investigating, of course, but let us just say that we have come across certain indications which *could* make it unlikely that they be of terrestrial origin. At the current stage, however, nothing can be ruled out."

"Mr Hogg, in my capacity as a science correspondent I've had more than a few people ask me about this particular subject and, tedious waste of time though it was, I looked into it long enough to be able to tell them without hesitation what I am about to tell you. There is no evidence whatsoever for the existence of alien craft, be they disc or cigar-shaped or black triangles half a mile wide; nor is there any proof that anyone except a gullible nitwit would give the slightest credence to the theory that extra-terrestrials, be they blonds or greys or humanoid giants, have made contact with human beings, be they world leaders or dyed-in-the-wool non-entities; or that said aliens have built undersea bases on this planet or any other; or that any of the contactees who have made a fortune by writing sheaves of twaddle about their supposed experiences complete with photographs of light bulbs attached to surgical lamps or scale models photographed using a double exposure, have been anything but shamelessly unscrupulous frauds; nor could I find any confirmation that the government of the United States or of any other country has been dismantling spaceships for the last half century in a process dubbed 'reverse engineering', thus giving the world such technological marvels as velcro and ballpoint pens that write upside down. I've looked them up, the contactees and abductees, and every single one of them has been debunked, from Adamski and his trees on the Moon and his unlikely mate Orthon from Venus, or the Italian Friendship group with their alien pals who looked like nothing so much as very tall Italians. In fact, I investigated the so-called UFO phenomenon until I grew so sick of it, I vowed I'd never bear it in mind again, as long as I lived. On which note, I believe I shall say goodbye."

I opened the door of the car and got out, slamming the thing behind me. He wound down the window in a hurry.

"Please, Mr Wyndham, this is a matter of life and death!"

I looked at his fearful face.

"Oh, piss off."

With that, I walked away but not fast enough to prevent him from catching up with me three cars along and thrusting a brown envelope into my hands.

"These were taken on an RAF base down in Somerset. It's because of them that I – and other people there too – are in danger."

A real nutter. Without a word, I left him standing there.

VI

When I got back to the flat, for some reason I wasn't able to put my finger on, I double locked the door before opening the envelope.

It contained a series of five 15 x 21 cm colour prints. The first showed a glittering grey disk sitting on a concrete floor. To judge from a section of wall to the object's right, it was housed in a tall building, possibly a hangar. The object looked as if it were about fifteen metres wide and some three metres high. The second, third, fourth and fifth pictures, taken from different angles, showed the same disc in the same place, only this time it was hovering roughly a metre above the concrete floor. From a technical point of view, it all looked quite interesting. I knew that the US and the UK – and probably the Russians and Chinese too – had been experimenting with saucer-shaped flying machines since the 1950s, so I assumed this vehicle must be some kind of military prototype. I'd always taken it for granted that the most reliable reports of unidentified flying craft were of man-made objects whose existence various governments wished to remain secret. Why Mr Hogg felt it necessary to hint they might be from outer space, I had no idea. And why on earth did he say that he and his wife, and even some unnamed others, were in danger? If he was working on a classified project, he would have signed the Official Secrets Act and been given a suitable security clearance. So there was nothing for him to be afraid of. I chucked the little pile of prints, face down, onto my coffee table.

Either that, it occurred to me, or he might simply be making the whole thing up, and that in real life, he was a grocer or a bank clerk. After all, there had been plenty of pathological liars, charlatans and con-men in the ufological world. Indeed, with a little help from any editor specialised in raster-graphics he could easily have faked the photographs he'd given me. And besides, if he really was working on a hush-hush government project, why would he risk losing such a lucrative job by giving sensitive material to a journalist?

I switched on my tablet. He wasn't on Wikipedia, and Google gave me nothing but dozens of entries for a long dead Conservative politician called Quintin Hogg. I tried a variety of sites and search engines and was about to give up when I decided to try Amazon. After all, long shot though it was, maybe he'd patented something, or written something, or designed something, that was on sale.

Quentin Hogg, and this did surprise me somewhat, turned out to be a children's author. He had three books out, presumably self-published by 'Whole Hogg Editions', featuring a little boy called Orthon – the same name as the fraud Adamski's imaginary Venusian friend – who took trips in a flying saucer piloted by friendly aliens. 'Orthon and the Sirusians'. 'Orthon

Goes to the Hidden Planet'. 'Orthon and the Mountain Chamber.' All three titles had been published over a decade ago and were over seven million down on the Bestsellers Rank. So, Hogg was doubtless a *frustrated* children's author. But one familiar with UFO lore. I shut down the tablet and hoped that would be the last I'd hear of Quentin Hogg, not to mention his addled wife, whom I assumed he had roped into his play-acting.

It was then I caught sight of the back of last of the pictures I'd tossed onto the table. It was stamped with the Royal Air Force logo, under which was a name: 'Weston Zoyland'. The base, presumably. Hogg had mentioned something about it being in Somerset. Irritated with myself, but feeling I had to do it, I switched the tablet on again.

Weston Zoyland existed, all right and yes, it was in Somerset; it had been used extensively by fighter squadrons in World War Two and during the Cold War. I googled some recent images. The airfield itself looked pretty run down, but there was one building whose windows were now covered with what looked like brand-new steel plates. Odd, I thought; then thought about it no more.

VII

The following Monday I was hard at work on a nearly-impossible-to-explain-to-a-lay-readership piece concerning the effect of dipole–dipole interactions on robot mobility, when I sensed someone standing behind me.

"It's six o-clock. Time to go."

"If I've got work to do, Adalyn, I stay on until it's finished."

"Not today."

I swivelled round. She was watching me in a very relaxed fashion for someone who'd just been so cheeky.

"Why not?"

"I thought we could have sex. At my place."

Never look a gift horse in the mouth.

"Your place? Outside of London?"

"Gravesend isn't that far. There's a fast train."

*

As we sat side by side on the High Speed 1's blue seats, zipping over the Thames's choppy dishwater, I wondered what she was up for. Straight sex, I took for granted: she'd offered it as if it were a glass of wine. But what more? A 69? Anal? Rimming? She pointed to the river.

"Water. I like it."

She did come up with the oddest things.

"Why's that, Adalyn?"

She looked surprised that I didn't know.

"It's life, Tim."

Eh?

"I don't think there's much life in the Thames."

"You're free to think what you like."

And by the time she'd come out with that non-sequitur, we'd whizzed through Northfleet and in what seemed no time at all were pulling up at Gravesend station.

*

We got into her car – a tiny, old-model Kia – which she had left in the station car park.

"It's a twenty-minute drive," she said, pulling away, "I live on the edge of town."

As we passed the shopping area, I couldn't help noticing that the car was as silent as a well-fed cat and – as she swung onto a main road that removed the river from sight – that the ride was exceptionally smooth, with not a bump or jolt.

"Forgive me for saying so," I said, "but this cheap South Korean banger is at least ten years old, yet it runs like a bloody Bentley."

She nodded, eyes on the road.

"I tinker."

Another surprise.

"You're a mechanic? Did a course or something?"

"More or less."

She drew up in front of a three-storey block of flats.

*

"The word for this, Adalyn, is austere."

And I could have added, a touch bizarre. The front door opened straight onto a living and dining area, which had three doors leading off it, and a wooden table placed in the middle with four chairs ditto placed around it. A TV screen was embedded into the far wall. Seamlessly, as I discovered when I ran a finger around its frame.

"Wow," I said, "this looks pretty state-of-the-art."

"It doesn't do anything except be a TV."

The walls were a dark blue and the table and chairs were a lighter shade of the same colour. It took me another moment to discover how the room was lit (which it was the second we walked in, so I supposed the flat used sensors, like the toilets in upscale restaurants); the lights, too, were flush with the walls. They emitted a warm light with just a dash of blue in it. But what surprised me most was the carpet, which was soft, yet looked like it was made of some kind of metal. I crouched down and touched it with my hand; it felt like a crew cut.

"Would you like some Armagnac?"

Adalyn was essaying a smile. I stood up.

"You have some?"

"Of course."

She opened one of the doors leading off the main room and we stepped into a compact kitchen consisting entirely of brushed stainless steel fittings: the cooker, the cupboards, the dishwasher, the sink, the sideboard, the fridge, all looked as if they had just been unboxed: there wasn't so much as a crumb of food to be seen on the surfaces. She opened the fridge, empty except for two bottles, one of Armagnac and another of Frangelico. She opened one of the cupboards, took out two glasses, put them on the sideboard, and filled one with my favourite tipple and the other with hers. Right there in the kitchen, she raised her glass:

"Cheers."

I confess I found her unusual way of doing things, interesting.

"Bottoms up."

In what I hoped looked like a spirit of complicity, I tried to down my drink as fast as she did hers. But, again, she beat me to it.

"This way."

I followed her back into the living area and through one of the other two doors into a bedroom, also carpeted with soft metallic hair, also lit from ceiling-high wall lights glowing a low blue. The bed, the only item of furniture in the room, was covered with a shiny silver coverlet.

"It's quite a place you've got here. Very original design."

Her placid face said:

"I pick and choose."

"So you did a course in interior design as well as automobile mechanics?"

I was trying to be funny, but even I could tell I sounded condescending.

"Take your clothes off and get into bed. I need the bathroom for a minute."

She went out, closing the door behind her. Her curtness suggested to me that she badly needed a good fuck. I shucked off my coat and slipped out of my Timberlands, my jeans, my button-down shirt, my black underwear. There was nowhere to hang or place them, and I didn't want her to come back and see me standing there like a wally, so I chucked the whole lot on the floor and got under the thin coverlet which turned out to be surprisingly warm. It felt like silk, but wasn't.

The door opened and for a moment I got a glimpse of her body or rather of her breasts, which were large but not too much so; before I could see any more of her, she flicked her fingers and the lights went out on the spot. You can't do that in upscale restaurant toilets, I thought, as I felt her slip into bed, but from the bottom end instead of the side, allowing her to climb directly on top of me. Within seconds I had a hard-on so taut, it hurt. She placed her groin over but not on it, leaning over me; I briefly touched those pumpkin-firm breasts.

Briefly, because she immediately straightened herself up and lowered her pussy down over my cock until my erection was fully encased. I was about to start pumping her when she placed her hands on my belly – they felt chilly – to still me. And then she did something that astonished my penis: she massaged it with the walls of her vagina, applying pressure on the tip first, then on the shaft as a whole, then on the root of the shaft alone, before returning to the glans, where she began to somehow shift the foreskin up and down inside her. After five minutes of this, I came inside her, more plentifully than on any other occasion I could recall (how banal, how anodyne did all the interns I'd been shagging for years seem in comparison!). Only then did I realise Adalyn hadn't said anything about precautions – it was usually the girl who mentioned the subject first – not that I had much time to think about that, because her vagina muscles were already kneading my receding dick back into a second erection and after a few more agonisingly ecstatic minutes into a second coming. I groaned, I moaned, I whispered her name; she stayed silent. I felt her slip off me, back over the bottom end of the bed.

"You can get dressed now."

I heard the door close and her fingers snap on its far side. The light went on, still tactfully dimmed. I got dressed. I was trembling. I felt drained, literally, as if I had not a homunculus left inside of me. Although there had been no foreplay, no dirty talk, and even though my contribution, as it were, had been minimal, I knew then and there that I had just experienced the one fuck I would remember until the end of my days.

Adalyn reappeared in a fetching if opaque gold-coloured nightdress.

"Are you all right?"

What an odd question. I bucked myself up.

"Never felt better."

"There's a taxi waiting for you downstairs. If you leave now, it'll get you to the station in time for the 10.15."

From my sitting position on the bed, I saw the front door opening behind her. More domotic tricks.

"You don't like making breakfast?"

She shook her head. The thinnest of smiles indicated that she had interpreted my comment as a joke.

"I have things to do."

She always did. I looked once more at her perfect skin, her naturally brilliant red hair. Twenty-seven? Really?

"I'm on my way."

She stood aside to let me pass. I expected to be allowed to give her a kiss on the lips but her head made no move in my direction. So I settled for a question instead, on the threshold.

"There's something I don't get, Adalyn. You've done this flat up in a way that's as nice as it's original. And like I said, you commute in every day. You're obviously not short of a bob or two. So how come you're working as an intern at the paper?"

From her bedroom doorway, she said:

"Experience. Have a good trip back."

"I'll see you tomorrow."

"Yes, see you."

As soon as I stepped onto the landing, the front door closed itself behind me.

VIII

I spent the journey back trying to conceal a nostalgic boner from the woman sitting next to me and when I got home I didn't bother to shed my coat before getting a porn website up on the tablet and clicking on the 'redhead' category and then masturbating with an urgency so imperative it surprised me, but not as much as the time it took for me to come did: an hour perhaps – perhaps longer, I wasn't timing myself – as if all the actresses I kept switching to one after the other couldn't compare with the girl with whom I'd just slept – or 'slept' – with. Even after I'd finally come, Adalyn would not leave my mind, not for a second.

I couldn't sleep that night, and entered the editorial offices the next morning tamped down by tiredness. I sieved through a pile of readers' questions, chose one, and answered it thinking only of how I could get a private word with Adalyn, given that I no longer wanted to creep up to her workstation like the intern-stalker I'd once been. I couldn't get it out of my head that if the sex had been that good when I was completely passive, what joys might await me if we interacted on a more equal footing, what games we might play. In the end, I decided that if Mohammed couldn't go to the mountain then the mountain etc. I emailed her.

'Could I have a quick word with you?'

'What about?'

Office emails, supposedly as private as emails everywhere, were prone to inspection from curious colleagues unless binned immediately after reading.

'Work.'

Within seconds, she was standing next to me, her perfect breasts concealed under a cashmere sweater, her legs wrapped in designer jeans, her red hair swept back into a ponytail, a sketch of a frown on her face.

"What is it?"

Said calmly.

"Adalyn, when would it be convenient for you to meet up again?"

She didn't hesitate:

"I think we should leave things be for a couple of weeks."

A fortnight!

"But –"

"I'll let you know the exact day. And by the way, this has nothing to do with work."

With which she turned away and walked off, leaving me in a state of frustration that the immediate seduction of a half dozen other interns wouldn't have relieved me of.

My phone beeped. It was Mrs Inopportune once more. This time she'd attached a press clipping.

'Dear Mr Wyndham, please read this article posted this morning on the website of your own paper. Both Quentin and I knew Dan very well (as we did his family). I do not believe the police version of events. Dan was as fit as a fiddle. Read between the lines, and you will see that when I say my husband is in danger, I am not exaggerating. Sincerely, Melissa Hogg.'

I groaned, audibly. A couple of colleagues glanced over at me. I slammed a finger down on my trackpad, twice, and up came that deranged hippy's clipping.

> 'Professor Daniel Blissett, 61, an astrophysicist in government employ, was found dead in his Wells home after suffering a cardiac arrest. He had recently been working at the RAF's Weston Zoyland base in Somerset. He is survived by his wife Elsa and their daughter Shivani.'

Weston Zoyland: the same slightly unusual name that had been on the back of the photographs which Mr Hogg had palmed off on me.

I didn't want to reply, of course, but felt sure that if I didn't, she would waylay me again on my way to the tube station, like before, or maybe she'd even go so far as to try and trace me to the sanctuary of my flat. So, reply I did, with a view to *really* putting a stop to this, once and for all.

'Ms Hogg, it is not unusual for people in their 60s to have heart attacks, no matter how healthy they might appear. If you or your husband persist in pestering me with your tales of supposedly mysterious phenomena which are nothing more nor less than perfectly explicable everyday events, I will instruct my solicitor to press charges on the grounds of unnecessary harassment. Goodbye for good. Wyndham.'

I leaned back in my swivel chair, wondering what it was, exactly, that she and her husband were up to. Like so many others before them, they could well have cobbled together a load of book-length baloney about UFOs, complete with phony photos, and were now fishing, by hook or by crook, for an endorsement from a reputable science journalist such as myself in order to help sell their material in large enough quantities to pay off their mortgage or buy a Lexus, or whatever it was their money-grubbing little hearts desired. The more I thought about it, the more likely my hypothesis seemed.

But blow me if I didn't get the following back, a handful of seconds later:

'You should know that both Quentin and I have been trying to contact Mr Blissett's wife and daughter, to no avail. Their mobiles have been switched off and they are not at home. This is most unlike them and we are deeply concerned, but given that you are the very opposite of the kind of person I imagined you to be, I will not be contacting you for any kind of help in the future. Sincerely, Melissa Hogg.'

Thank Christ for that.

So Mr Blissett's wife and daughter were off the phone and incommunicado. Of course they bloody were, being, as they must have been, out of their minds with grief and shock. Why were Mrs Hogg and her husband so blind to the bleeding obvious?

However, even as I sighed with relief, I noticed that something was niggling me. To have forged the name of the base on the back of Mrs Hogg's photos *before* it appeared in the newspaper obituary, was highly unlikely. Q.E.D, Quentin Hogg, far from being a grocer or a bank clerk, in all probability did indeed work at the base in a scientific capacity. As had the late Daniel Blissett. But in what capacity, exactly? And what if those photos really had been of new experimental prototypes? If I could unearth something – anything – about them, I'd have an exclusive on my hands which would put more than a couple of feathers in my journalistic cap.

The obvious place to start was the hack who'd written the obit, so I keyword-searched the item in that day's edition and checked the by-line.

Oh, no. But I couldn't pass on an opportunity like this. Even if it meant grovelling to the bitch.

*

"Hi Cathy."

She was only a couple of years younger than me, with long chestnut-coloured hair, and was dressed, as was her wont, in a dark trouser suit. Today it was navy blue's turn.

"Ms Edge, to you."

Catherine Edge and her assistant – a girl with a beard (and a nose that looked like a jeweller's display stand) – had produced some of the paper's most searing and serious exposés, and formed the tightest two-person clique on the premises. If they could have circled their desks like wild west wagons from the rest of us, they'd have done so.

"What d'you want, Timmy?"

How was I to know that during our fairly-long-ago fling – which she, serious lover that she was, had mistaken for something lasting – I'd been banging the 21st century's answer to Andrea Dworkin, squared?

"I've been reading your piece on one Daniel Blissett. I didn't know you did obits."

Her assistant was trying too hard not to look our way.

"They normally get farmed out to a friend, follower or fan of the deceased, but as Professor Blissett didn't seem to have many of those and as the data on him was scarce, they asked me to dig some up. OK?"

She turned back to her screen.

"Ms Edge, could I have a word with you in private?"

She jerked her face up.

"About *what?*"

Her cool, lost.

"Re Blissett, I'm in possession of some information which you appear to have missed."

"*In possession of?* How impressive-sounding."

The girl with a beard sniggered. Cathy stood up.

"Outside. Five minutes."

And she took a vaper out of her satchel, no doubt by way of justifying her leaving the office with a bona fide prick like me.

*

"It's freezing out here," she said, as we stepped out through the main building's electronic doors, "what the fuck is it that you want?"

"As chance would have it, a colleague of Daniel Blissett is an acquaintance of mine. Him and his wife both, in fact. Very nice people."

"Get on with it."

"I have it on good authority that Blissett and this acquaintance of mine and probably more people too have been working on something very hush-hush on that RAF base. I was wondering if you'd heard anything about that?"

"Why the fuck would I?"

Always so friendly.

"If you were researching his biography you must've come across the project he was working on before he retired."

She vaped.

"Supposing I did, why the fuck should I tell you?"

"Old time's sake?"

I wish I could have plucked those words out of the air as soon as I spoke them. She glared at me.

"You've got so much fucking cheek it's a wonder anyone can see the rest of your face. You treated me like shit, Timmikins, something I am not about to forget in a hurry.

Which unpaid half-child are you fucking now? Who's the lucky victim?"

"I guess I'm not going to find out much more about Prof Blissett, so –"

"It's not a rhetorical question. I'm curious."

Another vape. Won't-take-no-for-an-answer eyes.

"If you really want to know –"

"I do."

"I'm seeing the new girl. Adalyn."

Speaking her name aloud made my balls hum.

"That redhead?"

"You're a bit of a redhead yourself, aren't you?"

"Auburn, Timmy, auburn. *Her* hair's like a fucking smoke alarm. That said, she looks a bit more on the ball than the others."

"She's older. Twenty-seven."

Why had I told Cathy that? She screeched a laugh.

"Twenty-seven! For you that must be like shagging a granny, Timmo."

I took this on the chin.

"I'd better be on my way."

Vape three.

"Before you're on this way of yours, are you *in possession of* more specific information about that hush-hush project of Blissett's? Perhaps from that colleague of his you mentioned?"

For the first time since we'd spoken, she didn't sound like she wanted to set a Dobermann on my crotch.

"A little. This acquaintance of mine even gave me a few photos of what I suspect is a prototype aircraft."

"Did he now?"

"That said, I'm not sure what to make of them. Or of him, for that matter."

"I never thought I'd hear myself saying this, but why don't we have a little chat?"

A turnout for the books, if ever there was one.

"Where and when, Ms Edge?"

"Tomorrow at five. The bar of the Rochester. You know that hotel?"

It happened to be one of my favourites.

"I'll be there."

"You'd better be. And I hope you're not wasting my time, Timmy. You did enough of that."

*

The bar of the Rochester hotel had art deco details and cushioned stools and a couple of nooks equipped with sofas and armchairs. In a nutshell, it was intimate and snazzy and impressed the girls no end, who assumed I was taking them, flatteringly, to some outrageously expensive place, which the

Rochester wasn't: a double bed cost about a hundred quid a night, and one night was all I ever needed.

When I got there, Cathy was already sitting in an armchair in one of the nooks, a half of lager on the table in front of her. I ordered a pint of cider at the marble bar from a barman in a bow tie and black waistcoat. I sat on the little sofa on the other side of the table.

"Hi there."

Absorbed by her mobile, she didn't look up.

"Did you bring those photos you mentioned?"

"Sure."

I took the brown envelope out of my rucksack and pushed it over to her. She laid the pictures out on the table in front of her, one by one.

"My, my, the things our government is getting up to. Have you had these analysed?"

"Not yet."

If scornful looks could kill, I'd have met my maker there and then.

"And you're the paper's scientific expert? Weren't you even the least bit curious? In a time when anybody can make images of, I don't know, dromedaries in Bermuda shorts piloting motorised surfboards, you might have thought it worthwhile to get these equally unusual images checked out."

"I've got a lot of work on at the moment."

"Where did you say these came from?"

"My acquaintance, who works at the same facility as the late Mr Blissett."

Cathy frowned.

"Why didn't he send them to your phone?"

I had to think about that, but not for long.

"Any app he used would be trackable, and his phone could possibly or even probably have been hacked. He and his wife were convinced that something dreadful would happen to them if it was discovered he was leaking classified material. But like I said, I got the impression they were both a bit nutty."

Cathy sat up straight in her armchair.

"What made you think that?"

I told her about the meeting in the specially purchased Renault Four, and about the Hoggs's suspicions that Mr Blissett's death wasn't as natural as it seemed and their belief that there was something sinisterly fishy about the sudden silence of the deceased man's wife and daughter. Cathy took a notebook and biro out of her satchel.

"I'll grant you, Timmikins, that they sound like an odd couple. But if what they suspect has a single grain of truth to it, then you've just given me a story worth telling. Who'd have thought you'd be of use to me, one day? Hand me over those photos."

She started jotting.

"I'm going to get these evaluated. Then locate Daniel Blissett's death certificate. Then try and contact his wife and daughter. Then try and find out just what is going down at the..."

She paused.

"...where were they working?"

"A partially restored RAF base called Weston Zoyland. Weston with an O. It's in Somerset. Near Bridgwater."

Cathy jotted a little more, snapped the notebook shut, put it back in the satchel, and pointed to the empty glasses.

"These are on you."

*

It's true that we were in the same neighbourhood as the newspaper's offices, and it's also true that she was walking away from us on the opposite side of the street, but I couldn't help feeling it was a bit of a coincidence that she was a stone's throw from the Rochester just at the moment when me and Cathy stepped out of it. And what was it that made Adalyn turn to us at just that moment, red hair swirling, lips pressed into a half-smile, one hand rising as she called out:

"Hello, Timothy."

Cathy murmured:

"Well, well, if it isn't your latest paramour."

Adalyn crossed the road and addressed herself to Cathy first, hand extended.

"I'm Adalyn. I'm helping out in the Finance section."

Cathy shook it.

"I know, I've seen you around the office. How's things, Adalyn? Are they treating you OK?"

"Yes, thank-you." Adalyn turned to me, "How are you?"

"I'm fine," I said, not quite truthfully. Adalyn nodded at Cathy, her eyes still on me.

"Do you wish to penetrate her?"

Cathy's eyes widened and my jaw dropped. It was a second or two before I managed to haul it back up again.

"*No*, Adalyn. We're colleagues, that's all."

Cathy snorted.

"Don't worry, I wouldn't let him penetrate me any more than I'd let him kiss me on the cheek."

Adalyn raised her hand.

"Goodbye, then."

And back she went across the road, heading in the direction she'd been going when she'd spotted us. Cathy was looking at me with a what-have-you-got-yourself-into look.

"You've bitten off more than you can chew. To say she's not your type would be the understatement of the millennium."

Yet all I could think of was Adalyn's vagina massaging my penis and of how much I longed for it to do so again.

IX

Two days had gone by, leaving, by my calculation, twelve more until Adalyn's two-week moratorium came to a close. Occasionally, I passed by her desk and said hi and would get back a tiny but for me tantalising hello. It was on my return from one of these all-too-brief exchanges that I found Cathy waiting for me in front of my computer, her trouser suit a deep purple. She wasn't unattractive, Cathy, and my memories of taking her from behind and of her riding me that flashed through my mind as I approached her were not unexciting. But she couldn't hold a candle to Adalyn. No sexual memories could.

Cathy held up the brown envelope I'd lent her.

"I had these put through every analytical mill known to woman, and contrary to what I expected, the depicted objects are real."

I sat down on my swivel chair. She pulled over the empty one next to me, pulled out the pictures, and placed the three that showed the saucer-like craft floating above the floor, on the table.

"Photo analysis also revealed that the floating ones were motionless, and I mean still as statues. So, tell me, scientific Timmy, now that we know there are no strings attached, how could they possibly be doing that?"

This bitch of an ex actually wanted my professional opinion.

"There's on-going research on new aeronautical propulsion systems being done in both the UK and the US. But I'm unclear as to the details. Not my field of expertise. But there *is* someone I could ask…"

Old Prof Simmons. It had been a while.

"Then do it. Meanwhile, in your inexpert opinion, do you think these Anglo-American scientists *might* have managed to build working prototypes with the systems you've mentioned?"

I looked at the pictures. If genuine, they *were* truly extraordinary.

"It's not for me to say. Beats me, to be honest."

Cathy placed a yellow slip of paper on top of the photos.

"Here's something else that'll beat you."

It was a death certificate. Mr Blissett's. I squinted at the thing:

"Cause of death, cardiac arrest, it says here. I don't see what's so unusual about that."

"Look at the signature."

The certificate had been authorised by a Dr Anthony Tsong at Bridgwater Hospital.

"So? Bridgwater's the nearest hospital to RAF Weston Zoyland. When Blissett had his heart attack, that's where they'd have whisked him off to."

"Oh, there's no doubt he popped his clogs at Bridgwater. It's the doctor, one Anthony Tsong, that worries me."

"What about him?"

"He doesn't work at that hospital."

"You checked that?"

Cathy put her face uncomfortably close to mine.

"What is it you think investigative journalists *do*, Timmikins? I also checked the UK medical register, and Dr Anthony Tsong *is* on that. He's a cardiologist with a private practice here in London. 6, Devonshire Street. Up you get."

She stood up.

"What?"

She placed herself behind me, shoved her hands under my armpits, and pulled me up out of my chair.

"For God's sake, Cath."

"Get your coat."

*

The receptionist ushered us into a waiting room smelling of expensive carpet and whose marble-surfaced coffee table was covered with recent issues of *Horse & Hound* and *Country Life*. We were the only people there, which didn't surprise me much: this being the address it was, there can't have been too many patients around who could have afforded the services of Dr Tsong. Five minutes later, the receptionist told us the doctor would see us.

Dr Tsong was sitting in a velvet plush armchair behind a desk that looked like it had been purchased at one of Sotheby's more expensive auctions, his back to a wall packed with fat reference works. The result of a mixed marriage – to judge by the understated Chineseness of his face – he was wearing a pinstripe that must have cost at least as much as a medium-sized motorbike. He didn't bother to stand up, so we sat down, uninvited, in the two chairs placed in front of his antique table. He turned to Cathy:

"I was expecting one patient only."

Cathy nodded at me.

"He's no patient. And neither am I."

She held up her press card. Dr Tsong peered at it, and smiled.

"I confess I prefer *The Times* myself."

"We'd like to ask you a couple of questions, doctor. Medical ones."

He seemed to relax a touch at this. He looked at his watch.

"Five minutes? We're very busy today, I'm afraid."

"We noticed. The waiting room was packed to capacity."

Cathy shot a warning glance across my bows.

"Doctor, we'd like to know how it is that you also work at Bridgwater Hospital."

He frowned.

"Bridgwater? Where would that be?"

Cathy took Blissett's death certificate out and flattened it out in front of him.

"It's in Somerset, doctor..."

She pointed at his signature.

"...as you surely know."

Dr Tsong took out a pair of glasses from his inside pocket and put them on so as to apparently see better.

"After all, there is," Cathy said, "only one Dr Anthony Tsong on the national medical register."

He was nodding.

"Ah, yes. This was a one-off consultation, a quick day-return trip. Which must have been why it slipped my mind."

"An NHS hospital summoned a private doctor from London to record a death by heart failure?"

"There was some doubt as to whether it was a heart attack or death by misadventure. They wanted a second opinion. I am, after all, a rather well-known cardiologist."

"What kind of misadventure might that have been?"

A pause.

"Do you know, I can't remember. Given that the deceased, at least in my opinion, had definitely suffered a straightforward cardiac arrest, I… I didn't dwell much on any alternative diagnosis."

He stammered, he actually stammered.

"There must be plenty of competent cardiologists in Somerset. At Bridgwater Hospital alone, there are three..."

She'd done her homework, I gave her that.

"...why did they ask for you in particular?"

He practically snapped back:

"They were unable to agree on a satisfactory verdict and one of them – who happened to be an old friend and former colleague of mine – recommended that they get in touch with me, on the grounds that my opinion would be conclusive."

That was the first thing he'd said that didn't sound like a white lie.

"Could we have the name of this colleague?"

"I'm afraid not..."

Another glance at his watch.

"...duty calls, I'm afraid."

A wan smile with that. He stood up, which meant we had to. As he walked us to the door, I asked:

"We've been told that Professor Blissett was in good health and had no record of heart trouble. So how –?"

He shooed my question away.

"The heart is a complex organ. It's unusual, but not at all unheard of, for it to fail out of the blue, so to speak. Good day."

*

When we stepped out of the doctor's Georgian house onto Devonshire Street's Georgian-house-lined pavement, for a moment I thought I saw the back of a girl I recognised only too well, disappearing round the corner. I stopped, and pointed at where the back had vanished.

"What is it?"

"I thought I saw Adalyn. Just there."

Cathy shook her head.

"Watch out, Timmo, infatuation can kill."

We walked on, keeping an eye out for a taxi.

"It couldn't have been; I mean, what would she be doing in this neck of the woods?"

"Maybe she's stalking you, Timmy."

One drew up.

*

No sooner had Cathy stridden into her corner of the office than she began snapping orders at the bearded girl.

"Find out everything you can about the past of one Dr Anthony Tsong – T-S-O-N-G – cardiologist, current practice in London. Ditto for the three cardiologists who work in Bridgwater Hospital, Somerset; look for any details that overlap with Dr Tsong. And while you're about it, see if you can organise a visit to that hospital, for me and this gentleman…"

Me.

She was taking this story as seriously as I'd ever seen her take anything, which was good for me, because with her and her bearded girl doing the donkey work, the better the story was going to be and the quicker it was going to appear. But the by-line was going to be mine and mine alone, complain though Cathy certainly would. Well, let her. This was my story and I was going to use it to raise my standing and my salary. To judge by her sudden bossiness, she'd assumed I was now little more than an auxiliary lackey. More fool her.

X

The next day, Cathy came over to my desk, again.

"The visit to Bridgwater's all set up."

"That was quick."

"Roger's good."

"Roger?"

"The one who's transitioning."

"Oh, her. I mean him."

"He's got a very forceful, masculine voice, which helps when dealing with NHS bureaucrats."

"The rest of him's got some catching up to do, if you ask me."

"I'm not. Have you had lunch?"

"Yes."

"Good, then we can leave now."

"*Now?* Don't you ever plan ahead?"

"The visit is scheduled for this afternoon, that's the only time they could give us. Every silver lining has a cloud."

*

She had an Audi four by four which I decided not to tell her suited her down to the ground, being pugnacious-looking and austere. As we pulled onto the M4, she said:

"One of the three cardiologists at Bridgwater went to school with Dr Tsong, so we can assume he is probably the 'old friend' and 'former colleague' he mentioned. A Dr Hammond."

A sports car cut her up and she slammed her hand on the horn for more than a few seconds.

"Fucking male drivers."

She accelerated, drew up level with the sports car – a classic Porsche 911 – pressed her window open and gave the driver her finger. Then overtook.

"Turns out Dr Hammond has been at Bridgwater for just under a year. Before that, guess where he worked?"

"I give up."

"He's spent almost his entire professional career working for the RAF; he's an expert in aviation cardiology."

"That's a thing?"

"Yes. As for Dr Tsong, we drew a blank. Nothing, zero, zilch. The Medical Register normally gives a doctor's qualifications, but all we found was his name and his General Medical Council number."

She'd stayed in the fast lane, and was, consequently, driving fast. Too much so for my taste.

"So we asked the GMC to run a quick computer check. They confirmed that Dr Tsong was on their files, then asked us to call back in ten, by which time, so they said, they'd have located his record. But when we called back, the same person I'd spoken to earlier came on the phone and said she couldn't give us any further information about Dr Tsong. Naturally, we asked why, and were told she couldn't tell us. Then she hung up."

*

Dr Hammond turned out to be one of those ghastly people who laugh frequently for no reason whatsoever. We interviewed him in his office, which featured cracked paint on its walls and a computer which looked like it had entered the world a few years before I did. We asked him if he knew Dr Tsong.

"Tony Tsong! Ha ha ha! Good heavens, yes. We met at primary school when we were four years old and ha ha ha! have been crossing each other's paths ever since, ha ha ha!"

I wasn't sure how much more of this I could take.

"Where did you work before you came to Bridgwater?"

His mouth formed an O and his eyes widened.

"The RAF. I'm not at liberty to give you any details, Official Secrets Act you know, ha ha ha!"

"But surely you can tell us what a cardiologist is doing working for the air force?"

"Ha ha ha! Nice one, Cyril! Just like anyone else, pilots can get cardiovascular disease or CVD as we call it, ha ha ha! But of course if a pilot has a cardiac arrest when he's flying a fighter, where there's no one to take over the controls, well, that can be bloody dangerous, excuse my English, ha ha ha! In a nutshell, my research dealt with prevention of CVD for aircrew. And more than that I cannot say, ha ha ha!"

Jesus Christ. I gave Cathy a look which, I hoped, said 'say something before I clock him one'. She obliged:

"Did you cross paths with Dr Tsong during your time at the RAF?"

"With old Tony? I'll say, ha ha ha!"

"Was he involved in the same kind of research as yourself?"

"No, no, ha ha ha! he was working for the RAF all right, in a different department, but in the same building. We'd run into each other in the corridors, have a coffee in the canteen from time to time, chat at the annual Christmas party, and so on."

"What was he involved in?"

Another O, more wide eyes.

"Of course, we were both working under the auspices of the MoD, but he never talked about what he did, and I did ask him, you know, ha ha ha! I got the impression it must have been some kind of cloak and dagger stuff because he never gave me so much as a single hint of what he was up to, even though we'd known each other for yonks. But then again, he was, is, a few notches above me in the cardiological world, you know. He's what they call an eminence, ha ha ha! So I supposed he was working on something a lot more important than my poor CVD."

"Why did you decide to get his opinion in the case of Professor Blissett?"

"Ah, yes, alas, poor Blissett. Well, I had Tony Tsong very front of mind, as he'd paid me a visit just a couple of days ago and -"

Cathy leaned forward.

"Excuse me, he came to the hospital before Mr Blissett had his heart attack?"

Dr Hammond looked alarmed.

"Like I said, a friendly visit. He told me he was in the area and thought he'd drop in to say hello. I ha ha ha! don't know what that's got to do with Prof Blissett, who was alive and well and working at Weston Zoyland when Tony made that visit I've just told you about."

He was getting a bit edgy. My turn to lean forward.

"After Professor Blissett *had* had his heart attack, why did you send for Dr Tsong? Weren't three cardiologists enough to confirm the cause of death?"

Dr Hammond's face started to twitch.

"It wasn't clear what had initiated the attack. The patient didn't have CVD or any other heart-related illness. We ran a blood test, and found a slight, ever so very slight trace of a drug which, due to its having been almost completely expelled from the body, took us a while to identify."

"Which drug?" I said, in my top professional tone.

"Ah, ha ha ha! I do believe it was Ajmaline."

Cathy gave me a what's-that? look. I shrugged. I can't be expected to know everything.

"Please do go on, Dr Hammond."

"Yes, so I thought of my old pal Tony Tsong, who, like I said, had worked for the RAF – and Prof Blissett was an employee at an RAF base – and Tony is a loo-loo-luminary in his field, and I'd just been chatting with him not forty-eight hours ago. So I asked him for this favour. And he did it for me, for which I'm ha ha ha! immensely grateful."

"What was his diagnosis?"

"He looked at the blood test results, pooh-poohed the idea that the quantity of Ajmaline detected could have been toxic, and came to the conclusion that the cause of the infarction was an unforeseen spasm of a coronary artery. As Prof Blissett had no history of cocaine or amphetamine abuse – which can cause such spasms – he came to the conclusion that this one was stress-induced. We tried to get hold of Blissett's wife to ask her if her husband had been showing symptoms of stress, but were unable to locate her. Most odd, ha ha ha! But we went with Tony's diagnosis anyway. It struck all of us that it was the most likely of all possible verdicts."

Cathy stood up, so I followed suit.

"Thank-you for your time, Dr Hammond, you've been very helpful."

The face-twitching stopped.

"I'm pleased to hear it, although what help I've been, I can't imagine, ha ha ha!"

Dear God…

*

Back in the Audi, she switched the heating on.

"Well, science expert, what did you make of all that?"

"The whole thing is pretty odd, if you ask me."

"I'd go one step further, Timmy. I think it stinks to high heaven and that we've barely reached the outer edge of the cesspit."

Always so dramatic, Cathy.

"That serious?"

"We don't know exactly when, but Anthony Tsong had once worked on something secret for the MoD and perhaps is still working on it, who knows?"

"But that's nothing but specu-"

"So let me speculate, Timmikins! Fuck's sake. He had had a security clearance that his laughing chum Dr Hammond didn't, and perhaps still has it, who knows? Then we learn that recently he paid a visit to Hammond *before* Professor Blissett's demise. Hammond himself suggested this was a coincidence, given that Dr Tsong happened to be 'in the area'. And what else is there in this 'area' that a former or possibly not so former RAF employee with a possibly still valid high-level security clearance would be likely to visit?"

"I'm not an idiot, Cath. The Weston Zoyland base."

"Bingo. Well done, Timmy!"

"There's no need to –"

She turned the ignition key.

"I think we should take a look at Weston Zoyland."

"To do what?"

"Nothing in particular. Just for jolly."

*

She parked at the end of one of the abandoned runways, along which we walked towards the cluster of derelict edifices from which Meteors and Vampires had once flown sorties. Lines of ragged grass peeped dejectedly out of the interstices between the concrete slabs. Time was getting on and twilight could already be inferred from the sky's greyness, which stretched unabated over the flatness of the airfield and the countryside beyond it. Maybe it was the increased cold; maybe it was the eight gravel-covered graves and off-white tombstones of the test pilots whose prototypes had crashed decades ago, their memorials lined up against a breezeblock wall; maybe it was a half-demolished building crawling with underbrush; or maybe it was the moss-brown anti-aircraft gun emplacements: large brick gums with their teeth torn out; or maybe it was all of this together which made me feel an unprecedented sense of desolation.

"What's that?"

I looked off the tip of Cathy's pointed finger, and clapped a hand over my mouth (something I didn't normally do). She'd spotted the big square building whose windows were covered with the steel plates I'd noticed when googling pictures of the base. It stood apart and looked like a kind of squat control tower, bereft though it was of any visible electronic equipment.

"For my money, it's the only building in use here."

"So let's take a look."

She strode off the airstrip and across the grassy, squashy ground dividing it from the building. There weren't any warning signs and there wasn't a guard in sight. She stopped in front of one of the ground-floor windows, and inspected the steel plate that covered it completely.

"It's as if it forms part of the wall. There are no rivets, no signs of welding."

And so there weren't.

"But there must be a door somewhere."

We walked around the building and found not a door, exactly, but another perfectly flush steel plate which was a vertical instead of a horizontal rectangle. No handles, no knockers, no buzzers, no automatic porters, no video door phone. Just four initials, engraved in black:

M.I.S.S.

"Any idea what that stands for? The name of some kind of scientific institute, maybe?"

"Not one that I've come across." I was beginning to feel uneasy: "Wouldn't it be better if we made a formal request for a visit?"

She tutted no.

"Now that we're here, we might as well fucking knock. There are only two possibilities, Timmikins: either they open it or they don't."

"Cathy, we're trespassing on government property."

"Don't be such a fucking chicken."

She thumped three times, hard, with her fist. There was no echo, no slight buckling; no sound at all in fact, as if she'd punched a piece of foam.

"That's odd..."

Gingerly, I put my fingertips to the surface. It *felt* odd.

"It could be one of the new alloys. There's been a lot of experimentation in that field recently. Some of the latest products are up to a hundred times more resistant than steel."

"Thank-you for that, Timmy. Well, I don't think there's much more we can do here for the time being."

We walked back onto the runway, retracing our steps along its bleak length.

"Who the fuck's that?"

A car was parked next to hers. A – or rather *the* – classic Porsche 911.

"That's the car you gave the finger to."

She frowned.

"How d'you know that?"

"It's a 1970s Porsche. Worth a small fortune. Can't be more than a dozen in the country. It was headed in the same direction we were."

"Carspotter, are you, Timmy? How blokeish of you."

"I'm not. It's just – forget it."

There were times when she really got on my tits.

As we approached, the driver's door of the Porsche opened and a tall man stepped out. He looked like a caricature of a hippy, with shoulder length hair, a brightly coloured faux psychedelic shirt – in this weather! – tucked neatly into pressed jeans at the bottom of which were a pair of polished cowboy boots. He held up a palm.

"Hi there."

An American accent. Cathy replied:

"Hi."

I said nothing. The man pointed, playfully, at her.

"That was a pretty rude thing you did, flipping me the bird back there."

"I'm..." she shrugged, "...sorry. I thought you were driving dangerously."

He dug into the back pocket of his jeans, pulled out a plastified card and handed it over to her. She looked at it.

"Oh."

"Advanced international licence. I'm safer on the road than most."

Cathy gave him back his licence.

"Jimmy Craddock."

I found it necessary to say:

"Tim Wyndham."

"Cathy."

Without quite knowing why, we shook hands with him.

"You guys have a good day, now."

He slipped back fast into the Porsche's driving seat, gunned the motor, reversed the car, spun it a hundred and thirty degrees and raced off in the direction of the main road. Cathy said:

"Who the fuck is *he* and what the *fuck* is he doing here?"

My unmade guess was as good as hers.

*

On the way back, Cathy drove at a more leisurely, almost thoughtful pace.

"When we get back, find out everything you can about this Ajmaline stuff. What it's usually prescribed for, what side effects it has."

"Will do, boss."

"Don't get lippy with me, Timmy. If we were in the army, you'd be a Lieutenant to my Major. Roger and I get top priority, always."

That may well be, Cathy dear, but you seem to have forgotten the type of man I am. Come to think of it, perhaps you never even noticed.

XI

It was memory that served me. After having examined all the clinical information I could find about Ajmaline, I recalled a news item way back when I was in my early twenties: 2019. A German nurse with a loaf-shaped head was accused of inducing fatal heart attacks in up to three hundred elderly patients in his care, by injecting them with overdoses of that particular drug.

I sent Cathy an email about this, and in a flash there she was, in the flesh.

"I suspected as much."

"What is it that you suspected?"

"It's obvious, isn't it? Blissett almost certainly didn't die of natural causes. I've told Roger to turn this into a potential homicide investigation."

I should have kept my big email shut.

"That's ridiculous, Cathy. Ajmaline *can* be used to induce heart attacks if injected in sufficiently large quantities, which is what that kraut psychopath did. But that's the whole point: the doses found in Blissett's body were too low for that. It's more likely he had arrhythmia, for which he'd have been prescribed a small amount of Ajmaline as a matter of course."

"I'm going to see if Dr Hammond was telling us the truth about the dosage, and if Blissett really did suffer from arrhythmia, and take it from there. We've also tried to locate

Blissett's wife and daughter, and believe you me, Roger and I fucking *know* how to locate people. But not one trace could we find. They've vanished into proverbial fucking thin air."

"Look, Ms Edge, this story – if it turns out to be one – is about the advanced propulsion technology that's being developed in a British government facility. I am not going to stand for you messing up *my* exclusive with a lot of melodramatic crap. You don't have any proof of homicide, you don't have a motive, and you don't have a credible suspect."

She wagged a schoolmarmish finger at me.

"You have no fucking idea what I have nor what I can get in the near future. I'm going to do this story my way. You can go on taking care of the strictly scientific bit, if you want, and we'll leave it up to Larry to see if it's worth including in the story. He always has the final word, and I for one know who he's going to give it to."

Larry, the editor-in-chief, the only man Catherine Edge ever deferred to.

She stormed off. Like I gave a shit.

I got on with trying to find out about M.I.S.S., which had somehow kept its initials out of Google's range. Companies House, however, managed to inform me that it stood for Morgtech International Supplies and Services. The address and company type, however, were labelled 'classified'.

"Timothy."

Breath with a tinge of cold to it, less than an inch from my ear.

"Hello, Adalyn."

"After work, I would like to fellate you."

I almost giggled.

"Your place or mine?"

"Mine."

When I turned, her back was already moving smoothly out of range. I checked my watch: ten minutes until clock-out time. Then my screen told me I had a new email, and I wasn't about to win any prizes for guessing who it was from.

'This message is strictly confidential: I've found out how to use disposable addresses. Another colleague of my husband is due to be retired today.'

Jesus Christ on his bicycle.

'So what?'

'We believe he will go the same way as Daniel Blissett. I know you think that I'm making a mountain out of a molehill, but please look out for his name in the news. Tristram Crabtree, research engineer at Weston Zoyland.'

What was it with these people? To get rid of Melissa Hogg, I tapped:

'OK'.

And stood up. Time for Gravesend.

*

Adalyn's flat was exactly as it had been before: the metal table, the embedded TV, the dark blue walls, the flush lights, the crew-cut carpet, all of it clean as a whistle.

And, just as before, she asked me if I fancied an Armagnac.

"I don't feel like anything that strong right now. Have you got a cold beer?"

The tiniest of furrows appeared above her blue eyes.

"You also drink beer?"

"I'm not the only one."

"Later."

Really, she was the strangest of girls.

"I know the drill. I go into your bedroom and get undressed, right?"

She shook her head, came up close, unbuckled my belt and yanked my jeans and underpants down to thigh level. Before you could say Jack Robinson she was on her knees and massaging my penis a couple of times before placing it in her mouth wholesale. What she did then felt ecstatic enough for me to slam my eyes shut as she seemed to simultaneously suck and lick without once freeing so much as a millimetre of my member from the grip of her lips. And when I came, in waves, she kept her mouth right where it was and swallowed every drop, going so far as to extract the very last ones so that when she withdrew, my prick was dry as a bone.

She stood up and smiled, sperm traces glistening on her tongue. She yanked my underpants and jeans back to where they'd been, and fastened my belt for me.

"You don't want me to do something for *you*?"

"Such as?"

"Well, go down on you, for example."

A flicker of concern flashed across her face.

"That is not a good idea. But next time, I'll make sure there's some beer."

I was all set to say something silly like don't worry, I'm not here for the beer. But before I could get a word in edgewise, she said:

"See you tomorrow."

And before I knew it I was back on one of the High Speed 1's blue seats, watching dark-brown houses merging into the dusk.

XII

Two days later, I spotted a bite-sized news item in one of the five papers I browsed through each morning: Tristram Crabtree had died in a car accident on the M5, the previous night. Elevenish. A run-in with a pantechnicon. The truck driver, one Mr Weeks, had been injured, and was being patched up in Bridgwater Hospital.

For a moment I thought of letting Cathy know about this, but then thought no, fuck her (as indeed I used to). All I had to do now was wait for Melissa bloody Hogg to send me an inevitable email. Meanwhile, I started to delve into Morgtech.

It took me some time to find out that the CEO was one Charles Morgan. So: someone with an ego big enough to shoehorn his surname into the company's label. That aside, surf though I might, I couldn't find anything else about this man, other than that he was an American (along with three hundred and thirty million other people). I mailed Cathy, asking, with all the politeness and flattery I could muster, to see if she could do me a huge favour and ask her and Roger to check him out.

Then it came:

'Dear Mr Wyndham, I hate to say I told you so, but tell you I did. First Blissett went, and now Mr Crabtree. This is not a coincidence. I wouldn't bother you so, if my husband weren't due to be retired next week. From

what he tells me, they are gradually closing down the facility at Weston Zoyland.'

'Ms Hogg, I will admit that Mr Crabtree's death is an unhappy coincidence, but nothing more than that. After all, car accidents happen, as do heart attacks. Besides, the fact that the driver of the other vehicle was hurt surely rules out any possibility of this being a deliberate homicide. If you are so concerned, and I have said this once and I'll say it again now, but won't be repeating myself in the near or distant future: go to the police. Please.'

'Dear Mr Wyndham, I can assure you the police won't help, quite the opposite.'

Then I had a wheeze.

'Can you tell me anything about Morgtech International Supplies and Services?'

'Dear Mr Wyndham, I can't tell you anything at all about them except that my husband has worked for this company, which is under contract to the MoD, for several years, but has never given me one iota of information about it.'

I confess I was beginning to question my own assurances to Mrs Hogg that the deaths of Blissett and Crabtree must have been a coincidence. They had, after all, died within a week of each other. And then there was Dr Tsong: those two visits of his to Bridgwater, one before Blissett's death, one after, were certainly suspicious. I wasn't about to jump to any conclusions, I wasn't going to go down the Hogg woman's hysterical path or Cathy's homicide-fixated one, but I did want to set my mind at rest. There was only one way of finding out if Crabtree really had been the victim of a road accident. I made a note of the truck driver's name, and got my coat.

"Going somewhere, Timmikins?"

"Nowhere I'd tell you about, Cathy darling."

*

I went up to the fourth floor of Bridgwater Hospital, headed straight for the door of the room I'd been told Mr Weeks was in, and knocked. No answer. I went in. The bed was empty and unmade. The tube of an IV bag hung, listlessly, from an infusion stand by the side of the bed. I opened the cupboard. Nothing. I went to the nurses' desk.

"Can I help you?"

"I was looking for Mr Weeks."

"Room 419."

"He isn't there."

"Just a minute."

She unhooked a nearby clipboard with a list of names on it, ran her finger down it, and frowned.

"Well, he should be."

She stood up, opened the gate flap and walked quickly over to 419. I stayed where I was. She reappeared seconds later.

"That's very odd."

She got back to her desk, and was about to pick up the phone, presumably to make some enquiries. I interrupted her.

"Could he have gone for a walk?"

She looked irritated.

"Well, he could have done, yes, he wasn't that badly injured. Some nasty bruises and cuts, and a fractured forearm. But nobody's supposed to leave their floor without telling a nurse, and there's no record of Mr Weeks having done that. Now, if you don't mind, I have to report this."

She was on the phone for five long minutes. When she put it down, she looked *really* irritated.

"It would appear that just a little while ago, Mr Weeks checked himself out of the hospital altogether."

"*What?*"

She shrugged and sighed.

"Legally, they have the right."

I walked quickly over to the lift bank and went back down to the ground floor, thinking maybe I could still catch Weeks on the off chance he hadn't yet made it out to the taxi rank. As I hurried to the main doors, I heard an irritatingly familiar voice behind me.

"Mr Wyndham, oh, Mr Wyndham! Ha ha ha!"

Christ, no. Out of politeness, I stopped and turned.

"Dr Hammond, I presume."

"Oh, that's very good, ha ha ha, 'I presume', ha ha ha! They told me you were here and I wanted to have a quick word with you."

"If it really is quick."

He came up, uncomfortably close.

"Quick as a flash, ha ha ha! I just wanted to say that when we last spoke, I made a mistake."

"A mistake?"

"A terrible mistake, ha ha ha! I believe I told you and your female colleague that my old friend Dr Tsong had been here not long before poor Mr Blissett had his infarction ha ha ha! But I'd got all muddled up, Dr Tsong did drop by here, but it was oh at least a couple of months earlier than I'd said, he came to see me oh way back when; he was never in the area just before, ha ha ha!"

"Not just before poor Mr Blissett had his infarction?"

"Exactly! Well, I won't detain you any longer, busy bee that you are, ha ha ha!"

I was wondering why he'd taken so much trouble to tell me what sounded very much like a conspicuous fib.

"Dr Hammond, is it really legal for patients to check themselves out? Just today a Mr Weeks, a truck driver who was in a serious –"

"Oh yes, perfectly above board, ha ha ha! There are over a thousand patients in this hospital, checking in and out all the time, day after day, week after week ha ha ha!"

With which he hastened into a side corridor.

*

When I got back to the paper, the fluorescents were casting deadpan light over rows of mainly empty desks. Here and there, the odd man, the odd woman, were hunched in front of their screens, typing faintly. Adalyn had left. Cathy and Roger the bearded woman were at their posts, side by side, conferring in mutters. I moseyed over.

"Got anything you'd care to share with me?"

Cathy didn't so much as glance my way.

"I thought we'd agreed to work separately."

I took a breath. We had and we were. I had no intention of telling her about Crabtree's demise or the truck driver who'd gone AWOL or Hammond's change of story which, in my opinion, was almost certainly a bare-laughed lie. All of this would end up in *my* part of the report, which was nearly complete. All I needed was to put a few more pieces of the puzzle together and Bob'd be my uncle.

"I was thinking about Charles Morgan."

"Oh yes, the man you ever so exquisitely asked us to look into for you. And why did you think we would do that, Timmy?"

Roger giggled girlishly.

"I confess, Ms Edge, that I badly need some biographical light thrown on this man in order for me to take even the tiniest of first peeks into his scientific activities which belong, as per our agreement, to my side of the story."

"As it happens we've done you that favour, Timmy. We've been digging away, but the excavation isn't yet complete."

"Oh, no?"

I was fishing. And I got my catch:

"No. In late adolescence and early manhood he belonged to no less than four far-right groups: America Above All, Democratic Action, Charter 33, and American Werewolf. The first two were registered as political parties whose main activity consisted of distributing supremacist hate literature, and the last two were little more than bands of neo-Nazi thugs. At twenty-four he joined the army, but was cashiered for his practice of extrajudicially executing wounded prisoners in Afghanistan. We couldn't find hide nor hair of him for the next decade and a half. Then he pops up in his mid-forties, as a consultant for a defence contractor specialising in military aircraft. From there he segues to being an adviser for a joint Pentagon–MoD project which is still so highly classified our requests for data through the Freedom of Information Acts of both countries have been refused on the spot. Then he goes off the radar again for eight more years, before reappearing in his early fifties as the CEO of Morgtech, a job he's held for the last five years."

I confess I was impressed.

"Well done!"

Roger snorted into her beard. Cathy tutted.

"We're not that desperate for your approval, Timmo."

I let this pass.

"You mentioned he used to work for a company that designed military aircraft. So I take it he's now doing the same thing for the RAF?"

"And the USAAF: Morgtech has registered branches in both countries. But what I really don't understand is how this man graduated from beating up people with dark skin to owning a company that gets major government contracts."

Roger piped up:

"There's a total of eighteen years that we know nothing about. We need to fill in the blanks."

"Well, I'm sure you ladies will do just that. Meanwhile, I'm going to answer some long-overdue readers' queries."

*

But I never got around to answering any because half-way to my desk, my mobile pinged 'Get on Cablegram'. Cablegram, at the time, was a new app which claimed to guarantee complete encryption. I downloaded it, and almost instantly received the following:

'This is Shivani Blissett, daughter of Daniel. If you want to know what's really going on, I can tell you. In person only.'

There followed a list of instructions: a full circle on the Circle Line, then over to Oxford Circus station on the Central Line, then out of a certain doorway there, and back in again through a different one, and then a final Bakerloo Line trip to Elephant & Castle.

*

The Tube was crowded, squeezing room only, with its usual smell of cloth and ash. At Oxford Circus, I stepped through the automatic gates and took the exit Blissett's daughter had indicated: Argyll Street.

"Hi there Tim."

Jimmy Craddock, he of the Porsche 911, was leaning against the wall, his jeans tucked into his shiny boots, a brightly coloured shirt partially hidden by an Afghan coat, his long hair framing a smile.

"What the –?"

Before I could finish he'd taken a grip, firm, of my upper arm and was guiding me into the pub next door.

"We need to have a little word, Tim."

The Argyll Arms was packed, but he pulled me through the crowd of quaffing patrons to a table at the far end, which was somehow still unoccupied, as if surrounded by an invisible cordon. As we sat down, one of the bar staff came over and placed two halves of bitter in front of us.

"There you go, gents."

I didn't remember ever being served at table in a pub before. Craddock raised his glass.

"Cheers, Tim. Kinda full, those tiny tubular trains. Thought I'd lost you at one point."

I was still taken aback by the American's presence. Craddock switched off the smile.

"Tim, I'm here to help."

He took a slow sip of beer. Pissed off, I refused to touch mine.

"Why would I need any help...?" I could think of nothing better on the spur of the moment than to pretend to look at my watch, "Look, I'm sorry, but I have an appointment."

"Now that's precisely the kind of thing I mean. You don't need to be going to any appointment. I mean, c'mon, you're a science guy. You don't want to be talking to anybody about stuff that doesn't concern you."

"You know where I'm going?"

"There's no such thing as an unhackable cellphone application, Tim, not if you have the know-how."

"You know who I'm going to see?"

"I do indeed. And you're not going to, Tim."

"Why on earth not?"

"Because you have no idea, *no idea at all*, of what you're getting into. It's time you started to retrace your steps. Go back to where you came from. Systems theory, Earth science, astronomy, anthropology, all that stuff. That's what you're good at. Stick with it."

"Just out of curiosity, what would you do if I chose to continue on my way?"

"To Elephant & Castle?"

Christ.

"Yes!"

"Tim, I'm the good cop. If you want to run into the bad one, well, that's up to you."

I didn't care for his tone at all.

"So, Jimmy from America, if you're a cop, who do you work for? The FBI? The CIA?"

He stood up.

"The drinks are on me."

With which, he walked out. My pusillanimous father, I reasoned, would have taken the hint. Well, fuck the hint. I waited for some ten minutes, then completed the last part of the journey. Unfollowed, as far as I could tell.

*

Nobody at all was expecting me at Elephant & Castle tube station. No malign policeman and, more to the point, no Shivani Blissett. I waited in the station long enough for the security guard to start keeping an eye on me, then took a stroll around the block, following a brick wall beyond which lay an empty tarmac yard and a small, abandoned office block. Rounding a corner into another street, I came across a run-down three-storey building, with dirty-looking net curtains behind dirty-looking glass. A sign on the door said:

KEYWORTH HOSTEL

The bottom corner of one of the net curtains fluttered up and the face of a South Asian girl in her late teens appeared in the space made. A first-floor window. No sooner did I look her way than the curtain fell back into place. Shivani Blissett? I thought not: the place might once have been a bed and breakfast, an on-going concern, but now looked more like a council-funded half-way house for the homeless. Or for immigrants. Or both. And the Blissetts were neither. What's more, if their husband and father had been working on a hush-hush project for the MoD, they'd have enough dosh to stay anywhere they chose. Perhaps they'd even managed to leave the country.

XIII

When I stepped into the office the next morning, Adalyn waved at me. I went over. Her lips widened in that not-quite-a-smile she so often put on.

"Are you free this evening?"

"For you, Adalyn, I'm always free."

She ignored that.

"I would like you to anally penetrate me."

So gently said that not even her nearest workmate heard. Unlike some men I knew, I'd always thought anal sex was overrated. But then again, perhaps with Adalyn...

"Your wish is my command."

"Six o'clock, at the railway station."

*

Back in her flat in Gravesend, she led me once more into the kitchen, and yet again opened the fridge, in which there was now a six-pack of Heineken.

"Beer?"

"Why not?"

As she separated a can from the pack, I glanced round the kitchen, whose brushed stainless steel fittings were as crumbless as ever. I wondered if she'd ever cooked here.

Certainly, there was never any food in the fridge, nor on any of the surfaces. I was about to ask her about this when my watch sent me a more than surprising notification from the paper. About Keyworth Hostel.

"Adalyn?"

"Yes?"

Oh, those blue eyes, always so calm but never cold. And that bright red hair, that looked as if it were close to alive.

"Could we watch the news for a moment? Before we go to bed?"

She paused. Was that wariness I saw flickering across her face?

"We had better go back into the main room."

And when we did, the seamlessly embedded TV screen was somehow already on and tuned into a 24-hour news station. I stared, transfixed, as I lowered myself into one of the chairs placed around the centre table: the image was astonishingly vivid, as if I were watching Keyworth Hostel burning from the opposite side of the street: I could all but feel the heat. The entire building was ablaze, smoke pouring from its windows, long flames licking their way up its side, indifferent to the jets from the firemen's' hoses. Flashback shots showed people streaming out of the building when the fire had barely started. The voiceover informed us that one person had died in the blaze, his or her identity as yet undetermined. Five more had suffered burns of varying degrees. A be-tied, be-suited spokesman for the Health and Safety Executive came on, saying that some residents claimed they saw two incendiary devices being thrown into one of the rooms. However, all options were being kept open, continued the spokesman, until a full government enquiry had taken place. A banner with a helpline appeared at the bottom of the screen. I copied the number onto my mobile.

The report was major news, and it was wreaking havoc with what was left of my equanimity. I told myself I shouldn't make a direct link between this incident and the fact that Shivani Blissett had instructed me to take a roundabout route to a Tube station that happened to be just minutes from the fire. And nor could I say for certain that creepy Jimmy Craddock's hypothetical 'bad cop' had anything to do with it; but too many clouds were now gathering in the back of my mind: the unfeigned fears of the Hoggs, the photos taken at Weston Zoyland, the deaths of Blissett and Crabtree, the presence of an American who claimed to be working with who knew who... and now this fire. The only way of knowing if it was linked to the fears, the photos, the deaths and the unsettling American, was to find out the name of the one fatality. I turned to Adalyn, who was watching the images on the screen with a passive but not aloof expression.

"What do you think, Tim? Could you penetrate me anally now?"

Sex on the brain, she had.

"Look, Adalyn, I'm sorry, but could we do the anal thing later? I've got to be somewhere else right now."

She blinked, which reminded me that she didn't do it very often.

"Tomorrow. Six o'clock, at the railway station."

It wasn't a question. And I didn't want to argue.

"Sure."

I leaned forward to kiss her on the lips, but she turned her head so that the kiss landed on her cheek, upon which she suddenly gripped my head so that my lips pressed into her skin. That lasted several seconds. Once released, I headed for the door.

"'Bye, Adalyn."

"Until tomorrow, Tim."

Said with such certainty, such tranquillity.

*

When I got back to the office I glanced over at where the Home News team had its corner, and sure enough, they were busy as bees with Keyworth Hostel, its flames wiggling away on their screens. I walked past Cathy and Roger who, oblivious to the fire, were calmly scrolling down a text of some kind and taking handwritten notes. I sat down at my desk, called the helpline and identified myself as a relative of Elsa Blissett née Patel, saying I was trying to find out if she and her daughter were safe and sound. I was put on hold for a good few minutes. Then:

"Elsa Blissett was admitted to Saint Mary's with severe smoke inhalation. I'm very sorry, sir, but she didn't pull through."

I injected compunction into my voice.

"My God. Is there any news at all about her daughter?"

"I've already checked, sir. Shivani Blissett has not been admitted to either of the two hospitals which are treating victims of the incident."

So, uninjured. I sent her a message through Cablegram but got back 'User not found'. I was staring at these three words when Cathy's head leant over my shoulder and read them too.

"Found out anything, Timmikins?"

I checked myself.

"No."

XIV

The following evening, Adalyn didn't offer me a thing, no Armagnac, no beer, nowt. As usual, her flat looked and smelled as if someone had just scoured it clean it from top to tail. She simply led me into her bedroom, unfastened my fly and massaged my penis until it was hard. Then, without her doing a thing, the room plunged itself into darkness.

"Kneel on the bed."

I did so, my feet near the pillows, my penis pointing in the direction of the door I'd been able to see a second ago.

"Move forward a little."

"Adalyn, don't you think we should use some protection?"

The briefest of pauses.

"That will not be necessary."

So I shifted forward on my knees, as sightless as if I'd been blindfolded. Then she grabbed my erection so fast it made me gasp and before I could think a thing, she had guided it into her anus, which ceded, sponge-like, until it had taken all of me inside.

"Give me your sperm."

I obligingly began to pump, wondering what kind of lubrication she'd applied and when she'd done so. It didn't feel or smell like vaseline or KY and the more I pumped, the stranger she felt, as if her sphincter had an unsettling, oyster-like life of its own. As I speeded up, she made her anus clutch me tighter and tighter, but without any pain, on the contrary, the pleasure quickly turned into a helpless ecstasy at the end of which I came more than I'd ever come into anybody, herself included.

After which I heard her slide forward on the bed. When the lights came back on, she was standing at its foot, already in her golden nightdress. I looked down at my now limp penis. It was paler than usual, as if bleached.

"You must be tired."

Now that she mentioned it, I did feel tired; no, drained; no, so exhausted that even buttoning my fly required an effort from hands and arms whose muscles might as well have been surgically removed.

"I am, Adalyn, I really am."

"The taxi I have ordered this time will take you all the way to your home. It has been prepaid."

I nodded.

"Thank-you. And remind me some day to ask you how come an unpaid intern can afford a cab from Gravesend to central London."

I hadn't expected her to smile, and sure enough she didn't.

"Thank-you, Tim."

Said in a way that almost felt warm.

*

While the lamplights flitted past, foiled by dark buildings, and as the taxi's door locks clicked shut when it was moving ahead and clicked back open when it came to a halt at a traffic light, I realised, surprised at myself, that I was starting to have some serious doubts about Adalyn. Until then I'd always been a sucker for the apparently indifferent, cold-fish type of girl: they had something attractively unavailable about them, even when they made themselves fully available, so to speak, and in my experience, they tended to make themselves more available than most women, meaning, simply, they weren't averse to doing things that most women didn't. But that night, the coldly available Adalyn's matter-of-factness had felt disarming, and the sex had had an oddness to it, a hurriedness. Maybe Cathy was right, and I'd bitten off more than I could chew. She should know: she'd been too much of a mouthful for me herself.

The familiar squares of South Kensington eased their way into view and my home beckoned, with its isolation and its TV and its books and at least one pre-prepared meal in the fridge. As the taxi drew up to my door, and the locks clicked open yet again, I managed to feel relaxed.

Then the doors, both of them!, were pulled open and two people clambered into the cab, one from each side. For a moment I feared this was the materialisation of Jimmy Craddock's bad cop or cops until I recognised – it wasn't hard – Melissa and Quentin Hogg sitting perched on the fold-down seats opposite me. The driver turned his face's fleshy profile to me:

"Everything all right in there?"

Whatever else they had shown themselves to be – irritating, pesky, infuriating, right-royal-pains-in-the-arse – the Hoggs had never made me feel the least bit threatened.

"I believe so."

The Hoggs had changed since I'd last seen them. She still wore her hair like it was trying to imitate a collapsed haystack and he still had on a suit that would have suited an off-duty clown, but there was a purposefulness about them that was new. He spoke first, fast and bitter:

"As you couldn't or wouldn't help us, we've helped ourselves."

She took over:

"Quentin was due to be retired tomorrow."

"But I beat them to it."

He patted down one of his bobbing clumps of hair.

"You see, we didn't want to spend the rest of our lives moving from place to place."

"So we left our house in Somerset and moved into a London flat, without telling a soul. There's someone there we think you will be interested in meeting. Can I give the driver an address?"

I was taken aback and intrigued and alarmed all at the same time, and before I could think the words, I was saying them:

"Be my guest."

"Guildhouse Street, please."

I leaned over and tapped on the plastic divider:

"I'll cover the extra cost."

Again, the fleshy profile.

"No need, sir. Everything's paid for."

The cab pulled away and rode surprisingly fast along the upper rim of Chelsea.

"Flats, you see, are safer than houses."

Quentin Hogg gave me a wan smile that didn't make him look like he felt safe.

"Any particular house?"

"Number one, driver, if you would."

We got out in an empty street with a bus station on our left and a row of terraced houses built of old, grey-brown brick. The taxi gurgled away. I pointed at number one.

"This isn't a flat."

"And we don't live there."

No sooner had we walked out of Guildhouse Street than I realised we were not far from the newspaper and very close to the Rochester hotel. The two of them followed a series of all-but-deserted backstreets that they seemed to know like the backs of their hands, until we reached a building ten storeys tall.

"Used to be a hospital," muttered Ms Hogg as she led me into a lobby appointed with a pile carpet, faux antique furniture and a burly porter sitting behind a desk.

"Evening, John," said Mr Hogg.

"Evening, sir. This a guest of yours?"

"He is indeed. Mr Wyndham, this is John, a member of our excellent team of porters."

"Pleased to meet you."

John looked me over.

"Welcome to Matcombe House, Mr Wyndham."

The Hoggs escorted me to a lift adorned with wall to wall mirrors. Ever so quietly, Melissa Hogg said:

"The porters are our first line of defence."

We went up to a third floor and as we approached a polished wood door, motion sensor lights illuminated us so brightly, I had to shield my eyes. Ms Hogg removed two keys and inserted them simultaneously into two mortice locks, one just above a central smart lock, the other just below. She turned the keys until they made simultaneous clicks. Mr Hogg tapped the smart lock's keypad and opened the door.

"Wait a moment while I disconnect the alarm."

He started tapping at a larger keypad attached to the hallway wall, just past the door.

"That connected to the police?"

"No," said Ms Hogg, "to the porter's lodge. There's always someone on, twenty-four hours."

She followed me in, then quickly closed the door behind me, which is when I saw it had four fat bolts on it, which she immediately pulled shut. I followed them into a compact living room whose closed windows had little white boxes fixed to the frames.

"What do *those* do?"

Another wan smile.

"Make a hell of a noise should anyone try to climb in. Up to 110 decibels."

I nodded.

"Looks like you've got your second, third and fourth lines of defence pretty much in order."

"Oh no," said she, unzipping what looked like a specially stitched pocket in her maxi skirt, "all of that together is the second line of defence." She removed a bowie knife big enough to gut a shark with and pulled it out of its sheath with startling speed. "This," she said, with that resolution which had changed her tone so, "is our third line. Picked it up in the Army & Navy; it's like Harrods, you can get anything there. Only cheaper."

Melissa slipped it back into its sheath.

"Our guest," she continued, reminding me that she'd mentioned one, "got in touch with us. Her mother had had the foresight to open a P.O. Box in London. Once we had rented this flat on the QT, we sent a note with the new address to that P.O. Box, just in case, us being old friends of her mother. Which is how Shivani found us. Come on."

I followed both of them out into a short corridor at the end of which Quentin Hogg knocked on a white door.

"Can we come in?"

A muffled yes. He opened the door and there, in a well-lit room (more white alarms attached to the window frames) sat a girl in her late teens with straight black hair falling down to just beyond her shoulders, light brown skin, and dark, wide eyes that were angry, frightened and tearful. I recognised her there and then. Melissa's voice softened:

"Shivani, this is the person we told you might be able to help us."

So she still persisted in thinking, did this woman, that I was a vocational saviour. Shivani stared straight at me.

"I know who he is. Saw him just before the attack."

I was finding it hard to keep my usual objective face on.

"I'm very sorry about your mother."

"Why?" she all but sneered, "You never met her."

"Can I ask you," I said, "why she decided to move you and her into that hostel?"

Her voice tense as ever:

"With our looks, she thought it would be easier to blend into a holding tank for immigrants rather than check in to a hotel, where you have to show real ID. At the hostel, we gave false names in bad English and spoke Punjabi to each other. It helped also that the warden was off sick, so it was the Eritrean resident-in-chief who took our details, pending the return of the white supervisor."

A curl of her lip.

"How did you get my number?"

"Melissa gave it to me."

"Did you recognise me from the window?"

"Sure. I'd already looked your newspaper up. You have a by-line with your face on it."

Which is how Mrs Hogg had recognised me at the start of all this. That bloody by-line.

"So why didn't you come out and say hello? Come to that, why weren't you at the station to meet me? You asked me to go there, after all."

"Mum checked my phone – she had a habit of doing that – saw my message and forbade me to meet you. Said it was a bad idea, 'cos we didn't know if we could trust you or not."

"Do you know how the fire started?"

"'Course I do."

The odd twitch had started to sneak onto her face.

"It was just starting to get dark. Mum was always on the alert, always checking the window. So she was the first resident to see them coming and she called me to the window: two men wearing parkas and dark glasses and beanies were heading straight for the front of the building. Mum started yelling – screaming, really – at me to get out of the building, to go downstairs and out the kitchen door, which gave onto the back. She was so worked up I didn't think twice, I ran down and out that back door and kept on running; I heard a crash of glass and it turned out that those men, whoever they were..."

Tears were now finding their way into her eyes.

"...had each thrown a firebomb into our room, and nobody else's. Which is why everybody else had enough time to get out of the building. Except Mum."

I was about to ask her about the text message she'd sent me, saying she could tell me about 'what was really going on', when she covered her face with her hands and opened her mouth to release howl after no-holds-barred howl. Melissa sat next to her and put an arm around her and said to me:

"Elsa didn't stand a chance."

I nodded, mouth dry, my thoughts slowed by an unfamiliar dizziness.

I could now no longer believe that everything that had happened in recent days were coincidences or accidents. I was in a flat that an SAS commando would have had trouble breaking into, listening to a mentally shattered teenager whose mother had been burned alive by persons unknown, flanked by two people who had been personal friends of two men working on a classified project who had died in what were now clearly suspicious circumstances. Mr Hogg took my arm.

"Let's move back into the living room."

I glanced back at where Shivani had dissolved into Melissa Hoggs's arms, shivering like she'd just come out of a sea, her howls muffled by Melissa's sleeve. In the relative peace and quiet of the living-room, I stared at Quentin Hogg.

"I've got to know. What exactly were you all working on in Weston Zoyland? What is all this really about?"

He shook his head several short times.

"I can't and won't go into any more details than I already have, Mr Wyndham. Besides, I believe my wife told you that the Weston Zoyland operation is being wound up."

Weston Zoyland. Eight gravel covered graves and off-white tombstones lined up against a breezeblock wall; a half-demolished building crawling with underbrush; moss-brown anti-aircraft gun emplacements like large brick gums with their teeth torn out; a feeling of desolation...

I pointed at him, noticing with surprise that my finger was a-tremble.

"You two wanted me to investigate this, didn't you? Well, if you want me to do that, I need all the facts."

"If I were to put you fully in the technical picture, it would place you in the same danger as the rest of us. And you'd be a very easy target, Mr Wyndham. If I were you, I would concentrate on what you already know, which should be quite enough for you to publish a credible story that might help some of us to survive."

Then and there, I realised what I had to do.

"I should go."

He smiled.

"Check the street's safe when you leave, Mr Wyndham."

I called Cathy from the lift.

*

The Rochester's bar, as I'd hoped, was all but empty and I managed to occupy the same nook Cathy and I had shared a handful of days ago. No sooner had I stepped out of the Hoggs' posh block into the lamplit street than I'd been on the lookout for anything or anyone threatening, which by this stage I suspected might take any shape or form: poison darts chucked by the neatly turned out teenagers who were walking towards me, trip wires slung across zebra crossings, radioactive pellets slipped into my coat pocket by the motherly-looking woman scurrying past...

So it was with relief that I ordered a cognac and plumped myself down in one of the nook's armchairs. I checked my watch. Half nine already, but this being a hotel bar it would surely be open long enough for me to say everything I needed to say to Cathy, who was, I noticed as soon as I raised my eyes from the dial, walking towards me, looking especially fetching today, her trouser suit being jet black and her leather overcoat bright white. As ever, she wore her light brown hair down to her nape in a style that was half bob, half bangs. No make-up. The closer she got, the more she frowned.

"You OK, Timmy? You look like you've seen a ghost or two."

"I'm fine. Let me get you a drink."

"I can get my own, thanks."

She sat down opposite me with a pint of lager and lime and glanced at my glass.

"Is that that Armagnac stuff you tried to ply me with on our first date?"

Oh, touché.

"No, it's just plain brandy. I don't even know what kind."

"Very unlike you, Timmo."

"I confess to being a little nervous."

"How unmanly."

"No jokes now, please. I can assure you I wouldn't have asked you here if it wasn't, well, let's say fairly important."

She put down her lager and lime, which is the closest I ever saw her come to being disconcerted. Trying not to sound or even feel guilty I began at the beginning, with Mrs Hogg's message about Mr Crabtree's death by lorry, and my subsequent second visit to Bridgwater Hospital where I hadn't found the lorry driver but had run into Dr Hammond, who'd insisted that he'd got the dates of Dr Tsong's first visit to Bridgwater all wrong.

"Hold it there, Timmikins."

She dug into her satchel, pulled out a tablet, drew up a blank page and began typing, pausing only to ask me to confirm the odd detail. Then she sighed, and reached out for her drink.

"What else?"

I told her about Shivani Blissett's text message, and Jimmy Craddock with his cloak-and-daggerish hints.

"That creep with the old car who accosted us at the airbase?"

"Yep."

"Jesus Christ. Who the fuck is *he* working for?"

I explained my visit to a hostel which hours later went up in flames, my taxi being waylaid by Quentin and Melissa

Hogg and Shivani's description of how two men had accurately lobbed two molotov cocktails into the room occupied by her and her mother.

She drank most of what was left of her lager and lime.

"Why didn't you tell me any of this before? The earlier stuff, at least?"

Because I wanted to steal a journalistic march on you, Cath.

"We were working separately on this story, remember?"

"That's right. Me and my team were doing the strictly investigative part, and you were going to look into the scientific side of things. Well, all this stuff you found properly belongs to *my* side of the story."

"I'm sorry."

And I was. A somewhat malicious sparkle in her eyes.

"Is this a change of heart, Timmy? Are you actually saying that in the end, you'd like us to work together on this?"

"I am."

And I was.

"Are you OK with me being in charge of this investigation?"

"Why not? This thing isn't going to move forward unless we pool our resources."

"Music my ears never dreamed they'd hear. From you."

"Spare me the digs, Cathy. It's been a day."

"Talking of sharing, we've managed to fill in the gaps in Charles Morgan's CV."

"You have?"

"Tomorrow. You should go home and get some sleep. Anything I tell you now will slip off your brain like water off a duck's fucking back."

She had a point.

XV

The next day the air was so cold, it felt as if it were trying to shave off my three-day beard. When I got to the office, I noticed Adalyn wasn't at her work station. But interns worked odd hours, so there was nothing unusual about that. I told myself. I reached my own desk, shucked my coat over the back of my chair, and went over to see Cathy.

"You said you had more stuff on Charles Morgan?"

Roger the girl glanced at me. Cathy said:

"Before we get onto that, there's something you said yesterday that got me thinking. Before the fire, Shivani Blissett sent you a message saying that she could let you know 'what was really going on'. What do you think she was referring to?"

"I haven't got a clue. Honest."

Cathy looked at me, doubtfully.

"So let's look at Mr Morgan."

She picked up a file.

"Pull up a chair. This is interesting."

I wheeled one over.

"Morgan joined the army but was thrown out for carrying out extrajudicial executions in Afghanistan, remember? Well after that he knuckled down and studied, got into Stanford University, ended up with a master's degree, summa cum laude, in astrophysics, and was then recruited by Stanford to do advanced research work. After several years of that, he moved into the private sector, working as a consultant for a company making advanced propulsion systems for military aircraft. Then, as we'd already found out, he was an adviser for that mysterious Pentagon–MoD project we don't know anything about and probably never will. After that, he worked at a number of government installations, all of them linked to classified research projects: an R&D centre in Virginia, and a military research institute in Washington."

"How did you get this information, if these were all classified projects?"

"Very good question, Timmy! You're obviously nobody's fool."

I sighed.

"There's no need to –"

"Because Mr Morgan hasn't worked at these places for several years, his name automatically goes on the historical records they all keep as a matter of course. But *just* his name, with no indication of his position or his line of work. He's also a hard man to see: so far, we haven't been able to locate a single image of him. But we've got another lead on him and this is where I think your ears are going to prick up, Timmo. Remember that when he was a younger man he belonged to several far-right groups?"

"Sure. American Werewolf, Charter something..."

"Etcetera. He left them all. But the thing is, his views didn't change because at some point between working on all those classified projects and founding Morgtech, he became involved with an association called Flagship Liberty."

"Never heard of it."

"Hardly anyone has. It's a hermetic little group whose website contains nothing but an unsigned mission statement which makes the White Aryan Brotherhood look empathetic. It's racist, anti-Semitic, homophobic and misogynist; or rather, it's all those things to the power of ten."

My ears did, indeed, prick up.

"How can you be sure he's a member?"

"One hundred per cent sure, we aren't. But given that Flagship Liberty's official site is so meagre, Roger took a peep at the Deep Web and found a video down there of Mr Morgan giving a talk to a meeting of Flagship Liberty members, which suggests he's either a card-carrying member or at the very least a sympathiser. But that video's password-protected. Roger's working on it."

She looked at me.

"Which leaves us free for today. Got any plans?"

"Yes, I'm off to Lancaster. Re which, I need those photos back."

She picked the brown envelope off her desk.

"Lancaster?"

I took the envelope.

"Remember the other day I said there was someone I could ask about these?"

"Vaguely."

XVI

When I was an undergraduate, Professor Simmons had been a good, articulate, up-to-date physics professor; at the same time, however, he had a habit of trying to ingratiate himself with young people by using slang that was embarrassingly out of date. As late as the mid-Twenties he was using words and phrases like 'hepcat' and 'clip joint', which those of us who looked them up discovered went back nearly a century. These cobwebbed attempts at hipness sparked off giggles from mouths quickly sealed by hands that didn't want any signs of disrespect shown for this otherwise affable gentleman whose personal passion was rocketry, a subject which had made him a minor national celebrity (a big deal in our young eyes). Philip Simmons had published a half dozen books on the subject, including a biography of Soviet engineer Sergei Korolev, a detailed account of the Apollo 11 moon landing, and a history of the run-up to the first manned trip to Mars.

Semi-retired as he was, he'd agreed to see me at short notice. As my cab from the station drove onto the futuristically-shaped campus of Lancaster University, built in the Sixties of the last century, I was reminded of the feeling I'd had, when first entering the place seventeen years ago, that I was walking into the science-fiction fantasy of a long-dead architect.

Simmons lived in one of the university's grace-and-favour homes: two-room flats kitted out for the elderly with multiple handles in the toilets and bathrooms.

"Well, if it ain't the Timster! How's it hanging, man? You haven't changed at all!"

Which was more than I could say for him. His hair had shifted from fair to a pessimistic-looking off-white and his face had gone from mature to downright wrinkly. He noticed my silence.

"I know, I know, I don't party as hearty as I used to. Cop a seat, dude."

I took the only other chair in the room.

"Great to see you, professor, after all this time."

"Oh," he waved a dismissive hand, "call me Philip, you old square. And it's good to see *you*, some of those articles you publish are really *bad*, man."

He smiled in a watery way that might or might not have indicated an onset of senility.

"Working on anything new, professor?"

"I've been putting together some skinny on the doodlebugs the Germans fired into London. My grandfather remembered them well. A howling sound, then dead silence, then bang, you're dead! Offed about ten thousand Londoners."

"It's funny you should mention rockets, Philip."

"Just plain old Phil, please. Chill, Tim, chill!"

"I've obtained some photographs I'd very much like you to take a look at."

I pulled Quentin Hogg's envelope out of my coat pocket and handed it to him. He pulled out the five prints and examined them, cursorily at first, and then, stiffening, he brought each one so close to his face they were all but scraping the tip of his nose.

"Are these genuine?"

"To the best of my knowledge."

"Where do they come from?"

"A government facility in Somerset."

He coughed.

"We all know that various parties have been experimenting with alternatives to rocket propulsion, that is to say, to Newton's Third Law. But I'd no idea things had got this far."

"So what is it, do you think, that we're looking at?"

He sat back and took a short breather.

"The pictures of the craft in a floating, static position are especially interesting. They indicate that the craft has somehow created its own magnetic field, that is to say, its own personalised internal gravity system; and that same system enables it to feed off Earth's gravity in order to hover and perhaps even practise other manoeuvres. In theory. Of course, I can't tell very much just from these few snapshots. At all events, these are remarkable images. Really kickass."

I clamped my hand over an emerging giggle, not least because I wanted to ask him a question I never thought I would ask anyone, ever.

"Professor, Philip, Phil... please don't think I've gone crazy or anything like that, but there's something I have to check with you. These craft, are you sure, and I mean absolutely sure, that they're man-made?"

He stared at me, not getting it. Then doing so.

"Don't be so loco, compadre. Why shouldn't they be?"

"Well, because of their similarity to certain well-known photos purporting to be of, well, you know..."

"Every single one of those well-known photos was either a fake or a weather phenomenon or a planet or a prototype, Tim. You of all people should know that."

He slid Mr Hoggs' photographs back into the envelope.

"I do, I do, I just wanted to scratch the craziest possibility completely off my list of options."

He tapped the envelope with one liver-spotted finger.

"These must have been made on planet Earth, dude. But there is one thing..."

He handed the envelope back.

"...an autonomous gravitational field requires a great deal of energy to create and I haven't seen any visible housing for such a power source on these craft. It would have to be nuclear, which suggests that the people working on this have found some way of miniaturizing a nuclear power pack, just as years ago we found out how to miniaturize electronic circuits to a degree that would have seemed inconceivable to the previous generation. I'd love to know how they've done it, but I daresay the government isn't in any hurry to let us know. At all events, thank-you for letting me see these, Tim. Most exciting. Hot stuff."

He paused, scratched his ageing red nose. Then he started making a series of muffled huffing coughs.

"Of course," he said, "you realise that if you were to even mention the anti-gravity theory that I have hypothesised, an entire lifetime dedicated to advanced physics would go down the drain and that I would step into my coffin amidst guffaws of contempt emanating from the jaws of my eminent colleagues in the field?"

What could I say?

"Yes."

"Very good, then."

That was a cue. I stood up.

"Thank-you very much, Phil."

"No sweat, dude."

XVII

The next morning I checked Adalyn's desk. Still empty. I asked the person working next to her (someone I didn't know, he looked about eighteen, probably another non-wage slave) if she was due in today. He looked at me with a smidgen of disdain.

"I think she's left the paper. Didn't she say anything? I thought you two knew each other."

"Not well enough, apparently."

Cheeky sod. I wandered over to my desk, but didn't make it all the way because Cathy was waving to me, her face a picture of excitement, animated by a delight that went beyond the professional. A Cathy I hadn't seen before, not even when we were 'together'.

"Timothy! You've got to see this!"

I couldn't recall the last time she hadn't referred to me with a put-down diminutive. I hadn't yet plonked my arse down in the chair next to hers when she pointed to a jet-black screen.

"We found him!"

Eh?

"You've got to help me here, Cathy."

Her face went into astonishment mode.

"Charles Morgan! We've got a face and even better, we've got a speech, and what a speech! Headphones!"

I hadn't yet got them over my ears when she pressed Enter. A dimly lit stage appeared, with a man standing at a microphone placed in its centre. The audience, cast into blackness, was invisible, but I could just make out the outlines of the room enough to see it was fairly small, maybe a hotel meeting room, with space for maybe twenty or thirty people. The speaker was being filmed in profile, his face hard to make out until the camera, hand-held, swung round so it was at a three-quarter angle to the man's face, revealing him to be a fifty-something with rugged, pock-marked skin and hair cut conservatively, à la Cary Grant. From what the camera let us see of his body, he was wearing a black polo-necked sweater. A sound like waves slurping at the edge of a beach had me stumped for a moment before I realised it was applause. The man raised his hands, palms outward.

"Thank-you, thank-you very much."

A growl of a voice, à la John Wayne.

"To all of us who sail on the good ship Liberty, what I am about to say may well amaze you. It might even shock you!"

His stolid expression shifted into an overdone wide-eyed show of surprise. Respectful laughter.

"Indeed, I would go so far as to say that what I have to explain to you today will knock you for six. Or bowl you over, whichever you feel most comfortable with."

More laughter.

"My work has taken me to a very strange place, a place where at first I did not wish to be, until, upon reflection, I realised I had been bequeathed a privilege, a rare one, one which very, very few people have had the honour of enjoying. Gentlemen, I have seen and touched – not once but many times – flying craft whose provenance is not of this Earth."

He paused. Silence. Not a cough out of them.

"I do not tell you this as an amateur ufologist – come to think of it, *all* ufologists are amateurs – no, I tell you this as an astrophysicist who has been working with extra-terrestrial craft for a number of years. There are many things I am not at a liberty to divulge, but behind these closed doors, I am happy to inform you gentlemen that research is being done on the aforementioned craft with a view to reproducing some of their remarkable characteristics and features, for our own ends. Gentlemen, I kid you not, this will soon make the United States and its principal ally unbeatable in any future theatre of conflict you care to name!"

More slushing seawater. Louder than the applause of before.

"Jesus," I said, "they just lap it up!"

"Wait until you hear what he says next."

Morgan was nodding, and smiling without showing his teeth.

"There is nothing I would like better than to enter into further technical details, but those details are, as I have already intimated, classified above Top Secret. What I can do, however, is share a theory with you which I think you will find interesting. Those few of us who have been involved in the study and reproduction of the aforementioned flying craft, have not, I repeat not, had any contact whatsoever with the beings who piloted these craft. The craft in question were, so to speak, found objects. That said, I have been privy to the limited information that certain other people working for certain government agencies have managed to gather. It would appear that these Extraterrestrial Biological Entities, henceforth to be called EBEs – the word 'alien' should be reserved strictly for those foreigners who we would rather remained in their native countries..."

Laughter. A ripple of applause.

"…it would appear, as I was saying, that these EBEs are present among us."

That gave rise to a few murmurs.

"And it would also appear that they are not confined to one particular country or continent. Hearsay intelligence picked up by the government agencies I have just referred to would suggest that they are, as it were, a cosmopolitan race. And it is this word, 'cosmopolitan' which gave me my first hint, my first clue. It is an adjective that has often been associated with a certain ethnic-dash-religious group which is so dear to our hearts."

Another toothless smile. Laughter, but not much of it. The camera swung back behind his head until it was once more at a three-quarter angle, but focussed now on the other side of his face.

"What I am about to suggest to you may at first sound somewhat outlandish, but believe me, I have mulled this over for many moons and I am now convinced that my hypothesis is a reasonable one. So bear with me, people. I did some research and guess what I found? There is one group of people who have no known terrestrial origins, and there are no prizes for guessing to whom I am referring. Like so many guys, I kicked off with Wikipedia before getting onto the harder stuff. And what is the first sentence on the Wikipedia page that deals with the origin of the Jewish people? It states, and I quote: 'A factual reconstruction of the origin of the Jews is a difficult and complex endeavour.' End quote. I went on to do some in-depth reading, well, rather a lot of in-depth reading, to be honest, and discovered that the origins of the Jewish people are, in fact, shrouded in mystery. There are different theories, of course, ranging from the well-known but scientifically discredited biblical one, to the idea that the Jews originally formed a part of the Canaanite people, that is to say the people who lived between the Mediterranean and the river Jordan about six thousand years before the First Coming of Christ. According to the most reliable history books, it would appear that it took the Jews five thousand of those six thousand years to emerge as a separate group, with a religion of their own, though there is some disagreement about this among historians. In a nutshell, the jury is still out as regards the origins of the Jews.

"I did yet more reading, and it turns out that *there is no other single ethnic group on the planet* whose origins are so unclear. And not only that, but the behaviour of the Jews is and always has been similar to what we know or can deduce of the behaviour of the EBEs amongst us: the Jews, right from the moment they are first detected in Palestine, kept themselves very much to themselves...."

Morgan raised an emphatic finger.

"...very much! As if they didn't wish to mingle with the human populations that surrounded them. When they appeared in medieval Europe, they were, as we know, confined to ghettoes. But, it struck me, what if they weren't confined at all? What if they actively chose to live in the ghettoes, in order to maintain the same distance they'd always kept from people? What if their reputation for going their own way was not due to their being spurned by non-Jews, but a conscious choice? And what about the line they put out right from the start about being the Chosen People? Why all this isolationism? Could it be, I inferred, that they were engaged in some kind of activity to which they did not want other mortals to be privy?"

*

I shook my head.

"He's a total, complete, utter nutter."

"But," said Cathy, "as you said before, this particular audience is lapping it up."

*

"And no," thundered Morgan, "I am not suggesting that this activity was the usury which has traditionally been the trademark distinction between them and Christian folk. No, I am talking about something that only they knew about, that only they did and do. I began to suspect it involved some kind of research, research of a type that no human would or could undertake, partly because we humans do not have the means or the science, and partly because our morality would never let us carry out such research on, well, other human beings. And we know beyond a doubt that this research, involving the seizing and dissection of live humans, has been going on for years and years. It's in the literature, it's a documented fact, and has in fact been widely recorded in pre-scientific times, especially with regard to abducted children, as a Jewish practice, but we now know that this was not done, as was thought back then, for religious purposes, but for ones of research. Most of you will already have worked out where I am going with this. What if the Jews were not human at all? What if the Jews were human-like creatures from outer space? It sounds like a wild hypothesis, I grant you, but once I had framed it, everything, *everything,* gentlemen, seemed to fall into place. For example, take anti-Semitism, as opposed to Christian anti-Judaism. When did it appear? In the late nineteenth century, the great scientific century, the century in which we humans were pursuing hundreds upon hundreds of scientific lines of thought. What if the anti-Semites, perhaps intuitively, perhaps with who knows what tidbits of evidence, had started to suspect that the Jews were not like everyone else? What if the very Holocaust itself came about because the Nazis had discovered or even proven the alien nature of Jews, and tried so desperately to exterminate them because they considered them to be an existential threat to our own species?"

A pause. I needed a longer one.

"I see I have left you speechless. But when one gets a big idea like this, well, as I said, an indication that it is almost certainly correct is when all its pieces slot together like in a jigsaw puzzle. So, I propose that Flagship Liberty takes this idea on board, and begins to seed it, gently, subtly, to the larger population, with a view to creating an atmosphere, a mood, an undercurrent of thought within that population so that over time it will understand the need for defensive action to be taken. I leave you with that thought, gentlemen. Please hold it!"

He bowed his head. The applause that followed was crisp, loud and unequivocal. In the shadows, the figures of men rising to their feet could be made out. Cathy clicked stop. We took off our headphones and looked at each other.

"What do you make of *that*, Timmy?"

I shrugged and shook my head at the same time.

"There's nothing to be made of it. Mr Morgan may be a professional astrophysicist, and we know his firm is involved in classified research for the American and British governments, but it's also obvious as milk that he's a neo-Nazi nutjob who has a similar bunch of neo-Nazi nutjobs under his spell, something which must flatter his doubtlessly overblown ego. Who knows, maybe next week, he'll be telling them the Earth is flat and that the only reason we don't all know about it is because the Jewish aliens have somehow managed to keep the truth from us."

Narrow her eyes, she did.

"But Tim, that bit where he talks about research on extraterrestrial craft, that sounded genuine to me, which means that there's a possibility, well..."

"That they have a crashed saucer from Sirius 2? There is no evidence and never has been that Unidentified Flying Objects have come from anywhere other than Earth. The most publicised case – the supposed Roswell crash in New Mexico, you know the one – was a top secret operation involving a balloon used to track radiation from Soviet bomb tests. The abductions of people, to which Morgan refers in passing, have been proven to be hypnotically induced. Even the cattle mutilations that once caused such a fuss have been ascribed to natural predators in most cases, and to thrill-seeking sociopaths in the rest. But what definitively debunks everything that Morgan says in that speech, is the Jewish stuff. That's unadulterated bullshit."

Cathy clucked.

"So what is Morgan getting out of this? I mean, he's the CEO of a major defence contractor. He must be rolling in it and awash with prestige. So why have any truck with a lunatic fringe group? And why come out with such lunacy himself?"

I didn't have a bastard clue.

"I don't have a bastard clue, Cath. But, look, shouldn't we send this footage to the police? It qualifies as a hate crime, right? Who knows? It might even force Morgan to come out of his corporate bolt-hole."

"We've already looked into that possibility, but as the meeting was closed – in other words, not addressed to the general public – it's not a hate crime. And as it took place in the United States, if we had to alert somebody, it'd be the FBI. And they'd write off such weird racist drivel as beneath legal contempt."

She was probably right. There was nothing we could do with that footage, then, nastily bizarre as it was. My thoughts were already drifting back to Adalyn's empty chair.

"OK. I need to think this over. Let's touch base about this a little later."

I stood up. Cathy glared at me.

"Later? And just where d'you think you're going?"

"Private stuff."

"And I know which stuff. As Adalyn hasn't come in today, you don't know what to do with yourself, do you?"

"I just want to check up on her."

"And check if she's up for a fuck, if I know you. Jesus fucking Christ, Timmikins, we've got several suspicious, now *highly* suspicious deaths to look into, we've got a couple and an orphaned child hiding out in a fortified flat, we've got some fucking State-side creep following us around, and now we've got a Fascist head-case with a fat state contract preaching anti-Semitism and alien invasion to a group of people as much as or more unhinged than him, and you all you can think about is your penis's comfort zone. You haven't changed one fucking iota, have you?"

"Adalyn has something special," I said, and then added, just out of sheer bloody-mindedness provoked by being shouted at like a schoolboy, "as well as being the best lay I've ever had."

"Do me a favour: fuck off!"

Heads turned. I walked past the desks as quickly as I could, Cathy's voice growing thankfully fainter:

"Why I decided to work on this with you, I'll never know. Wanker!"

*

I took the High Speed 1, its blue seats all but empty at that time of day, me anticipating once more the excitement of the sex with Adalyn, the pureness of it, the singlemindedness of it, as I passed alongside the Thames, whose slight swirl put me in mind of being inside Adalyn's mouth, her pussy, her arse. But when I got out, and started the walk to her flat, the disturbing feeling I'd had the last time we'd had sex – that of being milked like a cow – started to scratch the back of my mind.

I rang the bell at the front door of her small block and the door clicked open at once. I walked up. The door of her flat was opened by a middle-aged woman with a pale, crinkled, round face.

"Oh," she said, looking disappointed, "I thought it was the builders."

Peeking beyond her, I could see things had changed. So I claimed that this had been my girlfriend's flat, that I'd left my phone charger behind and would she mind if I had a quick look for it?

"All right," she said, "but I'd appreciate it if you left before the builders get here; they're due."

"Much obliged."

All the light fittings, TV, silvery carpet and blue walls, had gone. The place had been stripped down, with peeling walls, bare floorboards, and not a stick of furniture, no table and much less the big bed. The fridge which had once held Armagnac, Frangelico and beer and nothing else, was also missing.

"Found what you were looking for?"

I shook my head.

"Must have left it somewhere else."

I thanked her – whoever she was – and got out of there.

I took the return train and let it pull me back into London. I slumped in my seat. I rolled into town wishing I was somewhere else. I didn't want to go anywhere, not to my flat, not to a pub and certainly not back to the paper.

Of all these unappealing options, the only realistic one was to go back home, where, at least, I could crash out, watch something on the TV or on the tablet, and maybe pretend to cheer myself up with a glass or two of, well, Armagnac. I got off the Tube at South Ken, dropped by the smarter of the local offies, purchased a bottle and headed over to the flat.

As both the latch and the mortice were locked, I wasn't expecting to find anything unusual, much less a floor covered with tossed papers, smatterings of wood, shards of glass. The TV screen had been cleaved in two, its innards spilling into each other and hanging limply off the wall; the single speaker had been unscrewed, its component parts lying in an unfixable jigsaw; whole sections of the parquet flooring had been upended; the armchairs had been cut open along the backrests, armrests and seats. And that was just the living room.

My bed had been stripped and its mattress sliced down the middle, cut pillows sprawled on its carcass. The kitchen cupboards and the fridge had had their contents raked wholesale onto the floor; the oven door had been removed from its hinges and left askew in the sink. There were no signs of my tablet. Whoever these bastards were, I thought, in a state of a helplessness both angry and fearful, they wouldn't find anything more work-related on it than they had done on the rest of the premises.

It was when I was staring, still in shock at the sight of the only place I thought of as home turned into a rubbish tip, that my phone rang, sending me swearing and digging into my jeans pockets until I found the thing. Who, in Christ's name?

The paper's landline number.

"Yes?"

"Timothy Wyndham?"

A deep voice I couldn't place. Not right then.

"Who is this?"

I'd barked that. I was, indeed, beside myself.

"It's Roger, I work with –"

"I know who you are, Roger; why the fuck are you calling?"

"Cathy told me to, Timothy."

"Why didn't Cathy get in touch herself?"

A yell.

"She didn't want to deal with you personally, Timothy."

"Don't you Timothy me. What is it?"

Arrogant bitch. Or prick, as he was becoming.

Cool as a cucumber, she – he – said:

"Some news has come in about the fire at Keyworth hostel. It'll be on the news and social media in a little while, but we thought you'd like to hear it first."

I took a breath.

"Well?"

"A far-right group has claimed responsibility for the fire-bombing. And, get this, it calls itself Charter 33 UK."

"So?"

"Doesn't that ring a bell?"

"Listen, Roger, the way things are at the moment..."

I saw now that two of my pre-prepared meals had been ripped open and their contents slopped onto the kitchen floor.

"...I'm not in the mood for any guessing games."

"Charter 33 was one of the neo-Nazi organisations that Charles Morgan used to belong to. It would seem they have a British branch."

"What?"

"33 is a reference to the year Hitler came to power in the last century. We ran a search on them, but of course there was nothing: no website, no social media accounts, nothing. But we don't think the name's a coincidence. So we checked, and according to reliable hearsay, Charter 33, alone among the neo-Nazi outfits in the UK, has been infiltrated by the CIA."

"Oh, *please*."

"That's what Cathy said. But she asked me to dig deeper into Charter 33 and all the other names that have cropped up in the investigation."

"Like Dr Tsong?"

"Him and Jimmy Craddock and Mr Morgan. We've found some interesting leads. I'm still digging."

She sounded like an efficient young fellow.

"OK, Roger, thank-you. My apologies for having snapped at you. I've got to go now. My regards to Ms Edge."

Now – looking around the flat – I knew for the first time how scared Melissa Hogg must have felt when she stopped me in Victoria Tower Gardens. This – or worse – is how Quentin Hogg must have felt when he invited me into his throwaway Renault Four. This is how they both must have felt when they sent me message after message and I replied like the prestigious, perfectly informed, sceptical journalist I believed myself to be; like the smug prig I'd been.

I opened the Armagnac, took a couple of swigs from the neck, hurled it to the floor and watched it seep across its smithereens into a mess of chicken korma.

Taking care not to slip on the kitchen tiles, I headed for the bedroom and checked the wardrobe. The jeans and jackets had been knifed open from top to bottom; my underwear and T-shirts, however, had been mussed up but left intact in their drawers. I pulled my suitcase on wheels out of its niche. Its top had been half ripped off the hinges. Useless. The coat I was wearing had two deep inner pockets, so I stuffed smalls in one and T-shirts in the other. By some miracle of oversight, my phone charger had been left intact in its socket, so I unplugged it and put it into a side pocket.

My thoughts were juggling disguised homicides, Jimmy Craddock, the CIA, hovering disks, Morgan growling his unhinged hypothesis, molotovs accurately thrown into a first-floor hostel room, the Hoggs holed up and defiant in their impregnable flat.

Their impregnable flat. With Shivani in it, shaking and weeping: the one person who had told me she could explain what was 'really going on'. Shattered though I was, one last drop of gumption, one final little rebellion against my father's habit of forever backing down asserted itself, assisted by a burgeoning rage against whoever killed Mr Blissett and Mr Crabtree accidentally on purpose, whoever told a laughing doctor at Bridgwater hospital to lie about the dates of Dr Tsong's visit, whoever used a spurious neo-Nazi cover name to set fire to the hostel in which Shivani and her mother were hiding out, and, last but not least, whoever trashed my flat. Whoever they were, well, *fuck all of them.*

I took the stairs down, and hailed a cab.

*

That entrance hall certainly was luxurious, its carpet muting my footsteps, its wood-lined walls smelling close to tasty. It was a relief, somehow, to see a familiar face at the porters' desk.

"Hello, John."

"Good to see you again, Mr Wyndham. Here for the Hoggs, I imagine?"

"You got it."

He waved at the bank of lifts.

"Up you go."

I couldn't help but notice – in the lift's wall to wall mirrors – that I looked harrowed, older even, maybe as much as forty. I stepped out and, transfixed like a startled boar once more by the flat's motion sensor light, I rang the buzzer. I was kept waiting for two or three minutes. I had my finger raised, ready to press the buzzer for as long as it took, when the door opened, but not much. Mrs Hogg's face appeared in the gap allowed by the chain, her tightly shut mouth visible below it and her eyes surly and cold, visible above its links. It took an effort to smile against these odds.

"Hi there!"

No reply. Her eyes were focussed on my neck.

"I wondered if I could have a quick word with Shivani."

"Shivani's not here."

A voice buttressed by impatience. My tongue fuffed around for words and found nothing but an echo of hers.

"Not here?"

"Ran off."

She wasn't expecting an answer. Her stare held on my neck for a couple of seconds longer before, knee-jerk-fast, she shut the door on me. Her expression had not been the one of tense purposefulness I had seen on her and Mr Hogg's faces when they'd stepped into my taxi and taken me to meet Shivani. And much less the intensely nervous one of the Melissa Hogg who'd come up to me in Victoria Tower Gardens. Her face now wasn't like hers at all.

I ignored John's friendly farewell as I headed out looking for a street busy enough to make a passing taxi a likely prospect. One passed.

"Where to, sir?"

Sir? I really must have started to look old. I didn't know where to. Somewhere with plenty of people. And pay phones, which I doubted even Jimmy Craddock could hack in time.

"Victoria Station."

*

Commuters pacing back and forth behind me, I made my call.

"What is it? Who is this?"

"Cathy," and it was only then that my voice started to tremble and my eyes to water and the hand that wasn't holding the receiver, to shake, "I'm afraid."

The silence that followed embarrassed me.

"Tim, are you OK?"

No snap in her voice anymore.

"No."

"Where do you want to meet?"

I hadn't mentioned any meeting.

"The last place, OK?"

*

How like home it felt, the Rochester, what with its oak panelling, its art deco lamps, its pure marble bar and its comfy cushioned sofarette, on which Cathy was already sitting over a pint of Guinness. I ordered a drink and sat opposite her.

"Thank-you for coming."

A look of surprise.

"You really *are* afraid."

"Why do you say that?"

"I recall certain moments of our ill-fated relationship, Tim, when you used to put on a poor-old-me act in an attempt to get back into my good books. You look a bit like that. Only much, much worse. So what happened that got you into this state?"

First I told her about my flat. Then about my unpleasant encounter with Melissa Hogg.

"What about Shivani?"

"I don't know. I find it hard to believe she would have left the flat of her own accord. It's not that Mrs Hogg sounded like she was lying, it's as if she didn't give a shit whether I believed her or not. She really gave me the creeps."

"Did she looked drugged?"

I thought of Melissa's eyes fixed on my neck.

"Maybe. Why do you ask?"

"Something I took note of last night when I was reading up about the CIA –"

"Seriously?"

"Please don't take me for some conspiracy-minded fucking Trot who blames the CIA for everything. But the fact is that we've already got some semi-reliable information that the CIA has infiltrated the neo-Nazi group that firebombed Elsa Blissett and Shivanis' hostel –"

"Roger mentioned something about that but –"

"Let me finish. And we've got Charles Morgan aka the CEO of Morgtech, who was closely involved in various sensitive military projects of the kind the CIA normally keeps tags on as a matter of course. And we've got that foul American who's been following us around, hinting to you that he's working for an organisation which could well be the CIA. Oh, and get this: Roger found out that the CIA leased the Weston Zoyland base from the MoD back in the 1970s, to use it as a 'supply facility'. As far as we know, they're still leasing it. But the research staff are from here, courtesy of the Ministry."

"All sounds pretty conjectural to me."

"Oooh, conjectural! Big words, Timmy!"

For god's sake.

"What about MI5? Wouldn't it object to the CIA stomping all over their turf?"

"It isn't unusual for the CIA to operate on British soil. They always ask permission from the secret services and they always get it."

I hadn't known that.

"Really?"

"Yes. So, like I said, I read up a bit about the history of the CIA and very interesting it turned out to be. They started off with very small-scale stuff, and ended up starting full-scale wars. Remember Vietnam?"

"Faintly. It cropped up in my history O level."

"In a nutshell, to carry out all these activities – or 'fun and games', as the Agency jokingly prefers to call them – it gradually built up a vast network of front companies, magazines and what have you, and – more importantly as far as we're concerned – infiltrated agents into hundreds of cultural and political groups."

"Like Charter 33?"

"Well done. It's an American organisation even if it does have a British chapter. Ostensibly they would have penetrated it just to keep an eye on its activities. Covertly – if the other organisations they've infiltrated are anything to go by – the CIA could have encouraged it to follow a CIA agenda, while allowing the agency itself to plausibly deny any involvement."

"The hostel attack?"

"It's possible or even, I'm starting to suspect, probable. Then I ran across something that might provide us with a possible explanation for the deaths of Professor Blissett and Mr Crabtree. Back in the early Fifties of the last century –"

"*Ninety years ago?*"

"Calm down, Tim. Another one?"

"I'm not sure what I ordered."

"Your thoughts were elsewhere, no doubt. Very understandable."

She took my glass and sniffed it.

"Since when did you start drinking Frangelico?"

Before I could say a thing she'd got up, ordered, and placed another glassful in front of me.

"Back then the CIA started a sideline in mind control, a now very well-documented project they called MK-Ultra, which involved handing out drugs like they were lollipops to their own employees, as well as to mental patients, prisoners, homeless people, prostitutes and Canadians."

"Canadians?"

"Don't interrupt. The CIA's main drug of choice was LSD. In the winter of 1953, the CIA invited one of their employees, an unfortunate called Frank Olson, to a retreat in Maryland and dropped acid into his bottle of Cointreau without telling him. Not long after that this Olson became clinically depressed, so the CIA put him up in a New York hotel pending a visit to one of their physicians. But before he got to see the doctor, he threw himself out of his tenth-floor window. This was in 1953. He was forty-three."

She'd lost me.

"Your point being?"

"MK-Ultra was investigated in 1975 and in Olson's case it found there was plenty of evidence to suggest that the CIA men who were with Olson in his hotel room had pushed him out of the window."

"But what's that got to do with -?"

"A couple of years earlier, Olson had been working on a chemical warfare programme which was secretly put into practice during the Korean war, something the US government has denied to this day. The CIA must have been concerned that in his unstable post-LSD state he might have let the cat of the bag. And so down ten flights he flew."

"You're saying that's some kind of precedent?"

"It's a very definite fucking precedent from 1953, Tim! Even back then, when my great-grandpa was pulling himself off to H&E magazine, the CIA were topping employees involved in sensitive military work. It's a fucking *tradition* with them. But in order to file we need unequivocal proof that something analogous took place in the cases of both Professor and Mrs Blissett and Mr Crabtree. And we haven't got that kind of evidence yet. We're not even near."

She bit that soft lower lip of hers.

"Now, as regards your recent brief encounter with Mrs Hogg: one of the reasons the CIA did all these experiments was to see if it was possible to control people's minds. Just to take one example, in 1954 a squeaky-clean airman who had no criminal record, raped and murdered a three-year-old girl he didn't know, then forgot all about it. Twenty years later it was discovered he'd been another MK-Ultra victim."

Melissa Hogg's bowie knife came suddenly to mind.

"Jesus!"

"What?"

"Imagine if the Hoggs had been given some kind of treatment like that...With a view to their getting rid of the Blissetts' daughter, Shivani."

Cathy thought about it.

"That's unlikely. So far, everything has been made to look like an accident or – in Mrs Blissett's case – a crime committed by someone else. But a murder committed by one or other or both of the Hoggs would attract attention to the Morgtech project; and that is the last thing that whoever is in charge wants to happen. On the contrary, they clearly want to keep it off everybody's radar."

She drank up.

"I've got to go, Tim. Can I drop you off at home?"

"No, I'm staying right here."

"In the Rochester?"

"I'm not going back to my flat until I've called the police."

"You haven't done that already?"

"I need a little time."

She leaned forward until our eyes were almost touching.

"You really do look shaken. Take it easy."

How I wished, by that point, that I could have just stuck with systems theory, Earth science, astronomy, anthropology, all that stuff.

XVIII

Three a.m. it was, when my phone beeped. A second Cablegram message from Shivani.

'Dr Song 9.30'

It was clear enough who she meant. I called Cathy on the hotel phone.

"It's three o'clock in the fucking morning, Tim."

"Have you still got the address of Dr Tsong's surgery?"

"Of course. Why?"

*

At nine a.m. sharp she picked me up at the hotel and we drove over to Devonshire Street. At a quarter past, she found a parking space six doors up from Dr Tsong's surgery. As we waited, I wondered what the hell we were going to do. Whatever was going to happen might get nasty and I'd never been one for a punch-up or even a scuffle. And I doubted Cathy had, either. Mind you, with her, you never knew.

Ten minutes later, Quentin and Melissa walked right past us, virtually dragging Shivani along by her hands. Cathy and I got out of the car. As the three came closer to the surgery, Dr

Tsong appeared on his top step. He grinned at the approaching trio. Then he spotted us behind them and was raising his finger to point us out when Cathy yelled:

"Shivani!"

Shivani's head turned, fear on her face. Cathy pointed to her Audi.

"In here!"

Shivani ripped her hands out of the Hoggs' grip and ran towards us as fast as only a teenager can. I opened the rear door that gave onto the pavement as Cathy slid back into the driver's seat and turned on the ignition. The Hoggs hesitated for enough seconds to allow Shivani to dive into the back. As they began to move, a mite sluggishly, in our direction, I slammed shut the rear door and plonked myself down onto the front passenger seat, closing my own door even as Cathy pulled away. We zipped past the Hoggs, who were turning their heads towards us, ever so slowly.

Whatever were they on?

Cathy swerved right – the first time I'd been in a car when its tyres squealed, film-like – and took Regent Park's Outer Circle at an arrestable speed. I looked round to where Shivani was crouching low on the back seat.

"Are you OK?"

"Thank-you, thank-you..."

She covered her face with her hands.

"Can we get you anything?"

She raised a tear-strewn face.

"Something to eat. Those freaks stopped feeding me."

Cathy took a sharp left. She was heading north.

"We're not taking her to the paper?"

"No fucking way."

"So where –?"

"Somewhere quiet."

A sharp left. She was heading north-west.

"Shivani's hungry."

"I'm not deaf. Shivani, can you wait a few minutes? I want to make sure we're not being followed."

"Yeah, sure."

Cathy didn't stop until we reached Chingford, where she checked her rear-view mirror several times before pulling up outside a corner shop.

"Get her something nice, Tim."

I came back with sandwiches, mineral water and cupcakes. Shivani didn't stop eating until Cathy had parked in a quiet street just off the eastern edge of Epping Forest. She nodded at the vegetation.

"This should be secluded enough."

We got out, looking around, then entered the woods. After we'd walked for a good quarter of an hour and had made sure there was nobody else about, Cathy said:

"So what happened?"

Shivani looked down.

"A couple of days ago, someone called at the door. Of course, Mr and Mrs Hogg didn't open it until they'd looked through the peephole and asked who was there. I heard a voice call through the door that it was a porter, they opened up, said a few words which I didn't catch with the man outside, then called out to me that they'd be gone for about an hour. When they came back, they weren't the same people at all. They talked in monosyllables and moved around like automatons, like they were stoned. They'd been very nice to me before, and now it wasn't that they'd turned nasty, exactly, they were just, well, cold. They started treating me like a pet they didn't want in the house anymore. They told me that tomorrow morning they were going to take me to a doctor for a check-up, but I didn't need a doctor, I was fine. That night they didn't cook supper, either for me or them, and that's when I knew there was something really wrong, because those two were very fussy vegans who made sure they ate at exactly the same time each day, to help their digestion, so they said. And now their quinoa and adzuki beans were sitting, untouched, in the cupboard. It was all so frigging *weird* that I decided to risk texting you."

"We're very glad you did."

We went on walking until we came to a tree whose roots were bulky enough for us to sit on, our feet washed by fallen leaves, our shapes shaded by soughing boughs.

"Shivani," that was me, "you sent me an earlier message saying that if I wanted to know what was really going on, you could tell me."

"That's because I overheard Dad telling everything to Mum."

"Everything?"

"About his work."

She sighed.

"The more you can tell us, Shivani, the faster we can go public with the whole story."

"So what?"

Snapped.

"So quite a lot. We could expose the project and the deaths and, hopefully, the people responsible for them."

Shivani looked at Cathy.

"Who are *you* anyway?"

"Cathy works for the same paper as I do."

"That right?"

Cathy nodded, dug into her satchel and handed her a business card.

"We're working on this together."

Shivani thought for a moment.

"Dad said he was researching a new type of aircraft. Some of the scientific stuff made sense to me, some of it didn't."

"I'm sure it'll make sense to Tim here. He's very scientific."

Cathy gave me a humourless grin. Shivani looked at me.

"You know what a graviton is?"

"Yes."

Cathy asked:

"What's a graviton?"

"It's a massless elementary particle in quantum physics. Like its name suggests, it accounts, in physical terms, for the force of gravity."

"Are you talking down to me, Timmy?"

"No! Go on, Shivani."

"These craft are powered by a rotating magnetic field, which in turn generates a beam of gravitons. This beam makes it possible to fold space-time, which means that point A, over London, say, and point B, over, I don't know, Beijing, are in exactly the same place. It's like the craft simply steps through a doorway."

Cathy frowned.

"Sounds a bit magical to me."

"No," Shivani said, getting into her stride, "because no rules of physics are being broken. These folds in space time are consistent with the Weyl curvature tensor."

Cathy looked at me.

"Hermann Weyl was a physicist who found a way to measure the curvature of space-time. What Shivani means is that these craft follow the paths laid out by this curvature. In other words, their technology – this gravity drive they use – is consistent with what we know about quantum mechanics."

"If properly developed, Dad said, this would give the West a huge advantage over its rivals," said Shivani. "I mean, they could arm these vehicles and have them pop up anywhere, and there's no way anybody could track them. They'd just appear, fire a missile or something, and vanish. At least, that's the theory."

Cathy looked at me.

"That chimes a little with a certain lecture we listened to the other day."

"What lecture?"

"It was given by one Charles Morgan, the CEO of Morgtech. Does that name ring any bells?"

Shivani nodded:

"Of course, he was Dad's boss."

"Do you know if he ever visited the research facilities in person?"

"Just once, Dad said. He didn't like him one bit."

"Were these craft supposed to make round-the-world trips, so to speak, or was the idea to get them to go further?"

"Like into space? No, Dad said. The originals can."

"The originals?"

Shivani looked at us, deadpan.

"Yeah, the *originals*. The ones that come from the mother ships, that are floating way out of range, probably beyond the limits of the solar system."

I didn't dare look at Cathy.

"Shivani, are you really saying that these craft your father and the others were working on, or trying to copy, came from outer space?"

"I'm only telling you what Dad told Mum. The whole idea of the project was to create replicas that could more or less reproduce the performance of the originals."

I'd almost had enough of this.

"Did your father say where these 'originals' came from?"

"He said they were recovered from crash sites in America."

"Did he say how many there were?"

"Two."

"What about the pilots?"

An effort it was, to keep any trace of cynicism out of my tone.

"Dad said nobody at the base ever mentioned anything about them. He thought maybe they got burnt up in the crashes or maybe there weren't any in the first place, that maybe those craft were remote controlled."

"And did he and his colleagues succeed in reproducing the performance of the 'originals'?"

"No, that's why he was telling Mum all this. He explained that the project had been a failure and it was due to be shut down and that he was afraid for himself and the other people working on it, as they'd been privy to so much secret information."

Cathy took out a vaper and began to blow out steam. I looked at her.

"It's been a while since I saw you doing that."

"I'd given up. Look..."

More steam.

"...I can't publish any of this so far. I'd be taken for a fantasist. Besides, it'd never get past the editor-in-chief."

Larry.

"So what do you suggest?"

"I'm going to sleep on it. Talking of sleeping," she looked at Shivani, "Why don't you stay at my place for the time being? You obviously can't go back to the Hoggs. And Timmy here has had his pad trashed by persons unknown. I'm your safest option."

Shivani looked at her for a few reflective seconds.

"OK."

Cathy turned to me.

"I'll take you back to the hotel."

What?

"Couldn't I crash out on your sofa? The Rochester's a hundred quid a night."

"The sofa, Timmy, would be too close for my comfort."

XIX

The following morning, I'd agreed to meet Cathy in the paper's staff canteen. She came over carrying a tray laden with a full English breakfast plus orange juice, coffee and bread and butter. I was nursing a cup of tea at a formica-covered table. The place was all but empty.

"Not hungry, Timmikins?"

"Nervous stomach. How's Shivani?"

She put the tray down. The whiff of burnt sausage and eggy bread and soggy tomatoes and beans in a bloodstain-coloured sauce made me feel nauseous and then, for some reason I couldn't put my finger on, sad.

"She asked me to lock her in. I filled up the fridge this morning before going to work. She'll be all right."

"My flat was raided. Why shouldn't yours be?"

Cathy brushed it off.

"You were the one who's been in direct contact with the Hoggs and Shivani. You've flagged yourself up, Timmo. It's true that I went with you to see Dr Tsong and the Weston Zoyland facility, but that's all and, knowing what most men are like, anyone watching – like the American creep at the base – probably assumed I was your secretary. Or your girlfriend. I'm pretty much off their radar, Timmy."

I wasn't so sure. Much as Cathy and I had never seen eye to eye after what I have to admit was a messy break-up, that didn't mean I wanted anything nasty to happen to her. I'm not *that* bad.

"You sound very certain."

"I am," she said, turning to the bread and butter, "as certain as I am now about the deaths of Crabtree and the Blissetts."

"By which you mean...?"

Cathy took the slice of bread back out of her mouth.

"They were murdered."

"You don't have any doubts?"

"No. Do you?"

I thought about that but not for long.

"Not any more."

"Very astute, Timmy. And what do you think about...?"

She stalled.

"The alien stuff?"

She winced.

"Well, yes."

"You know what I think."

She pursed her lips.

"Yes, and I'm inclined to agree. But how would you account for both Shivani's Dad and the Hoggs being so explicit about it?"

"Your guess is as good as mine. They could have been fed a UFO cover story, in part because if they believed it – and why shouldn't they have done so if, for instance, it had come from top-level military officials they were used to trusting? – they would have felt a sense of responsibility towards the public, not wanting to create any Orson Welles war-of-the-worlds type panic; or, alternatively, they didn't want to risk becoming the laughing stock of the scientific world."

"So why would they still be considered enough of a security hazard after they were retired, to merit assassination?"

"Maybe because some people who've been retired, no matter how many times they've signed the Official Secrets Act, have a tendency to whistleblow. Or maybe their research eventually led them into areas too sensitive to risk being revealed under any circumstances. At all events, I refuse to believe any alien bullshit that might have been dished out to those scientists, even if, like Professor Blissett and Mr Hogg, they *did* fall for it."

"And Morgan? He apparently believes in it too."

"Morgan is insane. It's a miracle he isn't in a safe ward."

"Can't argue with that."

Her finger tapped the table top once.

"So, perhaps it'd be wiser to leave the alien talk to one side for now. Perhaps for good. I'm going to see if Roger's been able to find out anything else. What about you?"

I sighed.

"I'm going to call the police about my home invasion. Then I need to finally get around to answering a few readers' queries. That's part of my job, after all."

"What do the readers want to know this week, Timmy?"

"The Pluto controversy is back again for the umpteenth time."

"What controversy?"

"About it being either a planet or a satellite."

"Yawn."

We took the lift up to the offices and I couldn't help but glance at Adalyn's work station on the way to my own. A common or garden intern had taken it over. Adalyn, it would seem, had gone for good.

XX

Back in my smashed up flat, the wreckage – the broken glass reflecting the listless white light from the street, the cloven screen which I used to watch with solitary pleasure, the spilling pillows, the shifted slabs of parquet, the dissected upholstery – made me feel helpless. The place smelt of unidentifiable spices: the food that had been sloshed onto the kitchen floor.

I was on the verge of not coping.

The buzzer went. I opened the door on two tall men, one of them wearing a burgundy-coloured crombie and the other a long black coat with artificial fur on the collar wings. They had pale, pasty faces. Black coat said:

"Mister Timothy Wyndham?"

"Yes?"

"Detective Inspector Willis. This is Detective Sergeant Donald. May we step in?"

Without waiting for an answer, they crossed the threshold together.

"I confess I wasn't expecting anyone from CID. Isn't this a job for the local constabulary?"

"We have it on good authority that this was no run-of-the-mill break-in, Mr Wyndham."

"I didn't give any details on the phone, so how –?"

Donald, he of the crombie, said:

"Heard it on the grapevine."

"Just so," said Willis, as the two of them looked around, "the grapevine. Gor' blimey. Didn't do things by halves, did they?"

He whistled. It sounded appreciative.

"Kitchen and bedroom through there, are they, sir?"

"That's right."

"Donald."

Donald veered off, kitchenwards. Willis took stock of the main living area.

"Doesn't half pong in here!" Donald called from the kitchen, "Don't employ a cleaner, sir?"

"I didn't want to touch anything. I mean, this is a crime scene, right?"

"That, sir," said Willis, "is for us to decide. Anything missing?"

"My tablet."

He stopped peering about and stood up straight.

"Anything on it that might have been of interest to the burglars?"

"I don't think so. Just personal stuff."

"Skin flicks, ay?"

"No. Just a few Filmin series that I've rented."

"Oh, they all say that, they do."

He grinned unpleasantly. I made an effort not to sound impatient.

"Look, do you think you can find out who did this?"

Willis snorted.

"My guess is as good as yours." He took another peek around. "But it looks personal to me."

"Personal?"

"You've been targeted."

Willis took a pencil from his inside pocket and began to poke about in the slaughtered upholstery.

"Wonder what they were looking for aside from the tablet. Any idea?"

"No."

"Anybody you know that hates your guts?"

"What? No!"

"Found anything, Donald?"

Donald appeared in the kitchen doorway.

"Chicken korma."

"Nothing else?"

Donald shook his head. Willis looked at me.

"If I were you, sir, I'd tread carefully."

His face was blank, his eyes, beady.

"I beg your pardon?"

"The person or persons who exercised such unnecessary violence upon your property, did so because they couldn't exercise it upon your person."

Donald joined us.

"That's basic criminal psychology."

"Indeed it is, DS Donald. Mr Wyndham, if I were you I'd take a little vacation."

"I beg your pardon?"

"A fortnight – at the very least – of sun, sea and a bit of the other."

Another disagreeable grin.

"But aren't you going to investigate this properly?"

Willis sniffed.

"We'll ask around. You never know, we might get some leads."

Donald said:

"Got insurance?"

I sighed.

"Yes, Detective Sergeant, I'm insured."

"I'd advise you to get the forms filled out pronto, sir. Otherwise it's going to cost you a pretty penny to get this place back to normal. I can tell you that for free."

"But bear in mind, sir," said Willis, "that you yourself can't be insured."

Donald nodded.

"No guarantees there. Better take that vacation we mentioned."

Willis added, with an air of finality:

"Meanwhile, like I said, we'll be asking around. You never know. We might get lucky."

Donald stood next to him:

"'Might' being the operative word."

They stepped back out onto the landing. Willis fixed me with those beady eyes of his.

"You take good care now. Sir."

A slither of a wink. A few minutes after I'd closed the door after them, my mobile rang.

"Hello?"

"You don't sound very chirpy. Haven't the Old Bill dropped by yet?"

"Yes, but..."

I couldn't work out what to say.

"But what? What happened?"

"They just left. A very odd couple. I got the feeling they weren't from Scotland Yard at all."

She paused.

"Who do you think they were, then? Didn't you ask them for some ID, for God's sake?"

"They were so fast and I was so taken aback, it never crossed my mind. I don't know, maybe they could have been from MI5. They were spooky enough."

"But you're OK?"

"More or less."

"OK, listen: Roger has come up with something else. Remember Weeks?"

Those things that days now felt like.

"Weeks?"

"Mr Weeks, the driver of the lorry involved in Mr Crabtree's road accident. The one who went AWOL at Bridgwater Hospital?"

"Right, him."

"Roger found out he worked for an Anglo-American trucking company called Long Range Transport. And guess who owns it?"

"The CIA?"

"Facetious though you sound, you're not far off. Morgtech International Supplies and Services."

"My God."

"Quite. Where are you now?"

"Home. In inverted commas."

"I'll pick you up."

"To take me where?"

"My place. I need to check up on Shivani. Don't take this the wrong way, but I'd feel safer if you came along."

*

Cathy drove us down to Brixton. I'd been there with her before.

"Still slumming it, I see."

She tutted.

"Don't be silly, Timmo. South London forever."

She parked on the zig-zagging street I still recalled the name of; we got out of the car, she unlocked her still-familiar blue front door and into the corridor we went.

"Take a seat. I'll make some tea."

She waved at the living room. I went in. Shivani was sitting on the sofa.

"How are things?"

She narrowed her eyes.

"How do you think?"

It was, indeed, a stupid question. Cathy came in with a tray holding three steaming mugs and handed them out. Shivani sipped. Then:

"The Hoggs got in touch."

Cathy and I sat up straighter.

"What?"

"They called me."

"Shit! I should have told you to disconnect. We know there are people involved in this business who can hack phones, who *have* hacked phones, which means they can locate you in the twinkling of an eye, no, that they probably *have* located you and you just happen to be *in my home*."

I was more concerned about the call itself.

"What the hell did Mr and Mrs Hogg want?"

Shivani held up her hands.

"Why are you both shouting? Look, the weird thing is that they were *worried* about me: in fact, Mrs Hogg sounded just like her old self again. So I asked her why they hadn't given me anything to eat for two days running, and why they'd taken me to see that doctor, but she said she didn't know anything about that, that they'd got back home yesterday and saw I wasn't there and were concerned about my safety. She kept on asking if I was OK, sort of fretting over me, all nervous like."

I looked at Cathy.

"That sounds like Melissa Hogg, all right."

"I almost felt like going back to them; after all, they'd been very kind and they were good friends of my parents."

"Shivani, listen, you can't afford to take any risks. There's only one thing that's going to provide you and everyone else with a watertight insurance policy, and that's that we get this story out. And now we finally can, thanks to everything you've told us about the project."

"But I don't want my name plastered all over the –"

"We'll say you're a reliable witness whose anonymity must be preserved for her own safety."

Cathy stood up.

"We need to move to a more secure location. Like I said, the call here to Shivani might have been traced."

"So that leaves just one option."

"We should buy shares in the fucking place."

XXI

Cathy booked her and Shivani into a double room – beige walls, roses on one table – in which we worked through the night while the girl slept, liaising with Roger at the paper, who stayed at his work station until the small hours. When we weren't texting Roger, we kept our phones switched off. Our first draft was composed on Cathy's tablet, and a very complete draft it was too: a case-by-case run-down of the deaths of Blissett, Crabtree and Mrs Blissett, with all the anomalies pointed out, chapter and verse; and seasoned, in the case of Professor Blissett, with circumstantial evidence taken from our notes on Dr Tsong and laughing Dr Hammond.

"When this is over, mind, Roger and I will be taking a good, long look at Morgan's racist ideas and his connection with Flagship Liberty. I suspect that could be a whole new story in itself."

When Shivani got up to go to the toilet, Cathy lowered her voice:

"When it comes to the craft, I think we should stick to that theoretical stuff Shivani explained, but avoid talking about the fact – according to Shivani's father – that the project was a failure."

"Why?"

"We don't have a clue as to what went wrong. We don't even know what the real aims of the project were. We'd be out of our journalistic depth."

"You have a point there."

"How gracious of you to say so. We could stick to the least crazy hypothesis: that the project involved work on highly experimental prototypes of new military aircraft, and leave it at that."

*

We took our time but we got there: we hewed our original draft into a four-page, fact-checked, watertight exposé. Charter 33, we now insinuated, needed to be investigated by an independent body. As did Mr Weeks and Long Range Transport. The final report allowed readers to draw their own conclusions, without actually accusing anyone directly. We decided to include the Hoggs in the story, but only up to the moment when I paid my first visit to their burgle-proof flat, when they were still behaving like their normally neurotic selves. As Cathy had put it:

"We can't yet account for the temporary change in them."

As for Charles Morgan, we decided to simply describe him as the CEO of Morgtech International Supplies and Services, and to provide the details we already had about his professional background, but without mentioning his batshit crazy speech.

It was around six a.m. and cup of coffee number seven when Cathy put a call through to Larry, our editor-in-chief, at his home number. She talked for a while, then put him on pause and looked at me.

"He wants us to file now."

"So file. That's a good sign, right?"

"Maybe." She reopened the line. "Give me a second, Larry."

She hung up, rooted around in her satchel, and took out a memory stick fat as a thumb. She winked at me, for the first time, ever.

"Bought this a couple of days back. Can't be too careful."

She didn't just copy our report onto the thing, she went through every separate piece of evidence, every recorded interview as well as the Charles Morgan video, until every last scrap of information was on the stick.

"Turn around, Timmy. I'm going to put this somewhere upon my person that will make it hard to find."

I turned around. Shivani – who hadn't – giggled, which was good to hear. Cathy finally filed the report from her tablet. Larry replied within seconds.

"He'll see us at eleven. Enough for a couple of hours' shut-eye. Shivani, you should come along with us."

"I still don't understand if this report of yours is going to name the people who murdered Mum and Dad."

A brittle, pressing tone.

"By inference, Shivani, by inference. Enough to kick-start a serious police investigation."

A tinge of doubt in her voice.

*

Larry worked on the same floor as us, in a circular office partitioned from the hoi-polloi by curved wooden panels that went up to shoulder height. He had a desk in there, of course, as well as a small, compartmentalised lounge area with a table and four spongily upholstered armchairs. I'd only met him a handful of times, enough to figure out that he was straight out of public-school central casting, his subdued voice mumbling close-to-verbose sentences which camouflaged an ironclad expectancy that everybody would carry out his orders, suggestions, hints and insinuations to the letter. Cathy deferred to him, all right, but I'd have let my right hand spend an hour in boiling oil if I thought for a moment that she had any regard for him. She knocked on the door, softly-softly.

"In you come, Cathy."

The three of us entered his Axminster-scented space. Larry didn't stand up.

"Ah, Timothy, you too. And, who might I have the pleasure of...?"

"This is Shivani Blissett, the daughter of the late Daniel Blissett."

"Enchanté, Miss Blissett. My condolences."

"Hello," she said, in too loud a voice.

"Please, let us repair to my little chill-out zone."

He stood up and opened the partition door that gave onto the lounge area. Jimmy Craddock was already rising from one of the armchairs, slow-clapping and smiling from in between the locks of his long hair, his brightly coloured faux psychedelic shirt tucked neatly into his pressed jeans.

"Hi there!"

Cathy and I were at a complete loss for words. He sat back down. Larry wheeled in his office chair, gesturing at the remaining three armchairs.

"Please, don't stand on ceremony."

We tried to make ourselves comfortable.

"To get the proverbial ball rolling," he muttered, "I'd like to say what a splendid piece of investigative journalism you have put together. I believe Sheila -"

"Roger."

"Of course, silly of me. Memory like a sieve. Roger has also been involved in your little project, is that correct?"

"Roger did some excellent research work for it. Shall I ask him to join us?"

A minute shake of the head.

"That won't be necessary. As you will see once Mr Craddock here has given us his spiel."

Spiel? Craddock turned to us.

"Thanks, Larry. And let me tell you guys, I fully share Larry's appreciation of the work you've done. That's one helluva good feature you all put together."

No thank-yous from us.

"Unfortunately, it won't be seeing its way into print – or online – anytime soon."

Cathy sighed.

"Always expect the worse."

Just who did this transatlantic bastard think he was?

"Why the hell not? The last time I looked, you weren't running this newspaper, Jimmy."

"And indeed I'm not, Timmy. I am merely the mouthpiece that speaks for people in echelons far higher than my own. Higher even, than Larry's. And these people have already reached a decision about this report."

"Do please," Cathy sighed again, "cut the crap."

Craddock's face broke out in a smile.

"Put simply, darlin', your article is too sensitive, too tricky. Hell, guys, if Larry published this he'd be letting one of the biggest cats our two governments have got, out of the diplomatic bag."

"Whereupon it could duly defecate large quantities of excrement all over the international stage," Larry added, launching into a series of muffled snorts which it took me a moment to recognise as chuckles.

"Larry, we have a moral right to publish. People have been *killed* because of the project we've been investigating."

Craddock's eyebrows rose.

"How come you're so *very sure* about that?"

"Let's start with Professor Blissett's so-called heart attack. We have good reason to suspect that his cardiac arrest was induced by a cardiologist and former MoD employee called Anthony Tsong."

Craddock nodded, poker-faced.

"I read the piece, darlin'. Talk about hearsay evidence."

"That might change if Dr Tsong is called in for questioning."

"It's never going to happen, Tim. Dr Tsong is currently on a sabbatical at a medical research centre in his father's native province of Shandong, as a guest of the Chinese Ministry of Health."

"What about Crab-?"

Craddock raised a staying hand.

"Mr Crabtree died in a car accident. In fact, there's a police report that says just that. And sure, the driver of the other vehicle checked out early from the hospital, the way some folk do. I've heard say he's not with Long Range Transport anymore, though he might well have been employed by any of the other dozen or so registered transport and freight companies which Morgtech owns around the world."

It wasn't hard to see where this was going.

"What about the Keyworth Hostel incident?"

"That fire?"

Shivani shouted:

"In which my mother died!"

Craddock looked at her.

"I know that, honey, and that was one helluva tragedy. And your very own British government determined that it was a vicious racist attack carried out by two perpetrators who are being sought after right now. From what I've heard, they've absconded to South America, where it might take a little longer to locate their whereabouts, but the authorities there will get them, have no fear."

"There are indications that Charter 33 is either CIA infiltrated or a CIA front."

Anger seething behind Cathy's quiet voice.

"Mere rumours, that wouldn't pass muster in a serious newspaper. Or in a court of law, for that matter. Plus I swear to God in high heaven that to the best of my knowledge the Company has not been involved."

"How come they threw the molotovs into mine and Mum's room only?"

"No need to scream. It just happened that way, little lady. Could have been your room, could've been somebody else's."

"You're lying!"

Cathy placed a calming hand on Shivani's shoulder.

"Why did Melissa and Quentin Hogg take Shivani to see Dr Tsong?"

"What I've been hearing is that they were, let us say, briefly encouraged to."

Larry raised some uncharacteristically surprised eyebrows.

"Whatever do you mean by that, Mr Craddock?"

I said:

"The CIA was looking into mind control as early as the 1950s, by handing out LSD to all kinds of people like it was lemon sherbet –"

Craddock dismissed my comment with a wave of his hand.

"My understanding – not that I'm an expert on the subject – is that the CIA has come a long way since then. I've heard say they can now persuade people to carry out very specific tasks and then erase those people's memories of said tasks."

"Are you saying that's what they did with the Hoggs?"

"I'm really not in a position to confirm or deny, Tim. But I can sure as poop assure you that the Hoggs these days are just as they were before."

"Before? Like when they were living in fear for their lives, as we reported?"

"Not any more, Tim. Not only are they back to their normal selves, they're not living in fear, mainly because there *is* no longer anything *for* them to fear."

How could he be so barefaced? I looked at Larry. Larry was looking at the tip of his shoe.

"How can you – I'm sorry, *they*, whoever they are – be so sure Mr Hogg's not going to spill any beans?"

"Because there aren't any beans left to spill. The project was not a success. As you so rightly state in your feature, it involved the development of high-speed airborne vehicles for military purposes. But Morgtech failed to achieve its objectives, so the relevant authorities on both the British and American sides ordered that the project be aborted. And you never heard me say that."

"What?"

"The research at Weston Zoyland is over. Finished, concluded, terminated, a thing of the past."

Cathy leaned forward.

"So what have you done with the remaining researchers, Jimmy?"

"Done? I'm afraid I don't catch your drift, Miss Cathy."

"I was wondering if they too were going to have fortuitous heart attacks, car accidents and the like."

"Mr Hogg was the last researcher working on the project. And like I said, he – and his wife – are doing just fine. As for the others, I've already made it quite clear that they, sadly, died of natural causes or, in the case of your poor Momma..."

He looked woodenly at Shivani.

"...in a terrible, deplorable incident."

"What about Mr Morgan himself? He's a major player in all this. Maybe even the prime instigator. He's held important positions in both governmental and private spheres. Oh yes, and he's a dangerous racist and anti-Semite. You can't tell me that he's just slipped out of the picture too."

Craddock seemed a mite surprised.

"The fact is, and you'll appreciate that I'm sticking strictly to the facts here, he's been under a lot of stress recently. So much so, that he had, well, if not exactly a nervous breakdown then something very close to one. He's currently recovering from it at an exclusive facility whose location is above classified for reasons which I'm sure you can well appreciate. It's not that you wouldn't be allowed to find it, Miss Cathy, you wouldn't even be allowed to try to find it."

She mulled this over, for a couple of seconds.

"All right, let's pretend that there's been no foul play and everything's just the way you've told it. So what about the craft themselves? We've analysed pictures, we've heard descriptions…"

Another supersized smile from Craddock.

"I don't know which photos you got hold of, but hell, any five-year-old these days can rustle up an image of just about anything in a matter of seconds. C'mon, you guys work for a newspaper, you know as well as I do that pigs have been able to fly for quite a time now."

Larry stood up.

"I do believe that, whatever the ins and outs of this complex subject, Mr Craddock has done us a service –"

I'd had enough:

"Service with a smile."

Larry glowered at me.

"– a service, I say, by coming over here to tell us in person why your otherwise excellent report cannot be allowed to find its way into print."

I stared at Craddock, aware for the first time of the extent to which I loathed the man. Cathy said:

"We could blog the story, Larry. Or try another publication."

A condescending smile.

"My dear Ms Edge, you know perfectly well that the appearance of yours and Timothy's article in any shape or format under any other banner than ours would entail the immediate termination of your employment for breach of contract; a breach, I might add, which would almost certainly lead to judicial proceedings on the part of this newspaper group that might have extremely serious consequences not only for your future careers but also for your respective bank balances."

Craddock stood up, looking at his watch.

"I hope you'll excuse me, I'm running late for another appointment. It's been a pleasure."

He shook Larry's hand – guessing correctly that he wouldn't be given a chance to shake Cathy's or Shivani's or mine – and headed for the door, but before his toes reached the threshold, Cathy said quietly:

"Who the hell *are* you exactly, Jimmy? Who do you work for? Surely you can tell us that?"

He paused.

"I'm sorry to be so blunt, Miss Cathy, but you really don't need to know."

Shivani jumped out of her chair and went for him, fists pounding his chest, one foot trying to connect with his groin. He raised his arms in mock surrender. Cathy and I had to drag her back. Off he went. Larry shrugged, and raised apologetic hands at the three of us:

"Sorry, chaps."

*

Over coffee in the canteen, Cathy and I decided to pay our second trip to Weston Zoyland. With Shivani, this time round: she'd never been there.

It was bleaker even than I recalled from the last time, what with winter settling in over the deserted runways and their now frosted tufts of grass; what with the test pilots' gravestones, the glassless brick buildings, and the remains of the ack-ack emplacements all looking more forlorn than ever.

"Wasn't *that* the building?"

It must have been, though without the metal plates sealing up the windows, it could have been mistaken for any of the base's other derelict structures. We walked over the mushy, green-black ground to where the door with the letters M.I.S.S. engraved in its centre had been, and where there was now nothing at all but a wide-open entrance. We went in.

Indoors, the walls and the floor were of smooth, grey concrete. We switched on our phone torches. The space was large enough to house half a dozen light airplanes. The scraping sounds made by our shoes echoed as we moved around.

"This was where Dad worked? But there's nothing here!"

Cathy shone a light against the foot of one of the walls. An Afro wig of coloured wires had bubbled out of a wide socket and sprawled over the stone.

"There used to be."

I looked around.

"I'm pretty sure this is the space where the photos of the craft were taken."

"Over here!"

Shivani was beckoning us from a doorway. We followed her into a maze of smaller rooms divided by glass and wood partitions. Here too, the electric sockets had been ripped out. There was a single toilet, whose cistern was dry. A few empty desks were still to be found in what must have been the office area. Shivani started to tug open the desk drawers, slamming them shut, peevishly, when she found them to be bare. And then:

"Hey!"

Cathy and I looked over to see Shivani holding up a silvery looking object she'd removed from one of the drawers.

"Bring your phones over here!"

We focussed them on what was a pizza-size replica of the craft I had been shown, what seemed like eons ago, in the pictures handed to me by Quentin Hogg. I rapped on it. It turned out to be made of plywood.

"Funny, it looks just like metal."

Shivani said:

"You have to sand it down then use metallic paint, then buff it carefully."

"Is modelling a hobby of yours?"

"It was one of Dad's."

I took the model from Cathy and held it up to our lights.

"Very detailed."

"You think Mr Hogg's pictures were made with this?"

"You don't?"

"No! I had them analysed back to front and from top to toe and they were declared genuine. Error-level analysis, level sweep, luminence gradient, you name it, we tried it. If a model had been used, that would have been spotted immediately."

"Well, it's true that that most vehicle prototypes start off as models," I held it up, "and then, once they're happy with the basic features, the design team moves onto larger versions. But all the photos show is that they managed to make the full-sized products hover a few inches off the floor. Not much to show for all that R&D."

Shivani piped up:

"But Dad swore to Mum that the original saucers came from another planet. He wouldn't have lied to her!"

Only then did I understand what had been going on all this time.

"Not lie, Shivani, but he might have told her a story in order to protect her. Something the government could plausibly disclaim, so that the real story, the real military project, would remain under wraps. Unfortunately, from what you've told us, he also gave her quite a lot of authentic technical details. Too many for her – and your – own safety."

"Never thought I'd say this, Shivani," said Cathy, "but for once I think Tim is right."

I was taken by surprise.

"Cross your heart, Cath?"

"And hope to die."

EPILOGUE

I informed my landlord that I was leaving my flat – which no longer felt like mine at all – at very short notice (that same day, in fact) and that he was welcome to the deposit. Given that the Rochester may have been affordable for a couple of nights but not for very much longer, I asked Cathy a second time if I could have the use of her sofa until I found another place to rent, something, I assured her, which it wouldn't take me longer than a week to do. She grudgingly acquiesced. That surprised me, but not as much as her suggestion, on night four, that I could sleep with her, if I wished. I wished.

It didn't take us long to recall what it was that we'd liked to do in bed, all the moves felt comfortingly familiar, and we ended up becoming a sort-of-couple, but without the rows we'd had the first time round. When I asked her why she'd had this sexual change of heart she told me that it was because I myself had changed, a lot. Not that she clarified in what way.

She had by then unofficially adopted Shivani, whose unofficial stepfather I soon became, which felt odd at first given that she was *almost* the same age as all the interns I'd been humping ever since I started working for the paper. But after a few weeks I came to see her as more of a grown-up daughter. Well, as good as.

We never heard anything more about or from Jimmy Craddock, or Charles Morgan, or Dr Tsong, though Cathy and Roger – who had by now become a believable man, to the extent that I soon forgot he'd been anything else – poked about on the internet for nearly a month. There were no traces of those people whatsoever, as if they'd never existed, as if we'd never talked to them, never seen them breathe.

*

After a month had slipped by, I decided to take the risk of dropping in unannounced at the Hoggs' fortified flat. A moment after I rang the bell, unlit by any motion sensor lights, Melissa opened, without any bolts being pulled back first.

"Hello?" she said, with a doubtful expression.

"I just wanted to see how you both were."

She was still looking at me as if I was a Jehovah's witness, but invited me in anyway. Quentin was sitting on the sofa in the living room, reading a copy of *Prospect* magazine. He stood up, looking as puzzled as his wife, who simply said:

"This gentleman would like to know how we both are."

"Oh!!" he said, with a confused shrug, "Well, we're both fine, thank-you."

The windows were open. The white alarms had gone.

"I was passing by and just wanted to make sure: have you been or felt threatened in any way in the last few months?"

They both stared at me with increasingly baffled faces. Mr Hogg took up the slack.

"Why, no. Should we have been?"

"Given what happened to you both last year, it doesn't strike me as being an unusual question."

Mr Hogg said:

"I'm sorry, but who do we have the pleasure of addressing?"

My turn to look baffled.

"Timothy Wyndham."

Melissa Hogg shook her head.

"I think you must have got the wrong door, Mr Wyndham."

They were both staring at me now, their bemusement laced with a touch of nervousness.

"You really don't remember me?"

"We do not, sir!"

Mr Hogg had come close to snapping. I raised my hands, palms out, to show I meant no harm.

"I'd better go, then. I'm glad everything's fine."

Silence.

"I'll show you to the door," said Mr Hogg, moving quickly over to me, followed at a short distance by his wife.

When he opened it before I could so much as reach for the latch, I said:

"By the way, Shivani's OK."

They looked as if they were trying to think.

"Shivani Blissett. The girl who stayed with you for a while."

They both nodded, without registering a flicker of recognition.

"She's OK, you say?"

"Thriving."

"Excellent," said Mr Hogg, in an I'd-like-to-get-rid-of-you-right-now tone of voice, as he closed the door behind me, quickly.

Jimmy Craddock was right: the CIA's mind control programme *had* come a long way.

*

Just one year past her teens, Shivani became engaged to a man from Goa, learnt Konkani, and – together with her new husband – divided her life between that Indian enclave and her native London.

As for me, I ploughed on, answering my readers' queries and writing up scientific discoveries whenever they rolled around. The years, too, rolled around, washing me up on the beach of my fortieth birthday in what seemed to be no time at all. It was at about that age that Cathy decided to Platonise our relationship because, as she put it – all but apologetically, and with a smile that might have been wry – she'd 'met someone'. A someone I myself never got to meet, who she ended up going halves with on a little house in Streatham. South London forever. I found a flat in Islington.

I don't know quite what it was I'd imagined my future would be like when I first landed my job as a science correspondent, or when I wrote my two fairly-good-selling popular science books, but at forty it started to dawn on me that although I hadn't done badly for myself, things weren't going to go much further and that that was my lot. By way of testing my future's water, I wrote a third book, but unlike the others there was little demand for it, something which made me desist from having a fourth go.

It wasn't as if I was thinking much about my own death at this stage, but let's say I could now feel it inching closer, enough for me to know without a doubt that when it finally came for me, it would find itself face to face with a retired journalist whose concluding years had been pretty much uneventful.

Unlike the autumn and the winter of that year when Cathy and I had stumbled across something so fascinating that it had chuted us down into a world in which the kind of people we had previously thought of as rumours, were doing things we hadn't suspected were possible. For those two seasons, my life stopped making much sense; and perhaps for that very reason, they would always be, I was sure, the time of my life.

That, at least, is what I was thinking when I wandered, lonely as a cloud, into a Cafè Nero on Wandsworth Road.

And saw her.

*

She was sitting on a booth bench that faced the entrance, with her un-made-up lips, her calm blue eyes, her pale and seamless skin and of course her electric red hair which might well have been taken for a wig by the uninitiated but which I knew perfectly well was very much hers. She was watching a little boy sitting opposite her as he dipped a spoon into a dessert I couldn't see. I ordered a latte and moved in her direction, not without trepidation, it having been a full five years since we'd last met.

It was only when I was within hand-shaking distance that she looked up and took in my presence as calmly as if we'd made an appointment.

"Hello, Tim."

That warm-cold voice.

"Adalyn! What a coincidence!"

All of this exclaimed too loudly.

"Would you like to sit in the same booth as us?"

Before I could answer, she had slid over to her right, leaving me a space smack opposite the little boy, who was digging his spoon assiduously into what I could now see was a chocolate mousse.

"So! How are you?"

"I'm very well, Tim. And you?"

"OK," I said, wondering whether she really wanted to know, "Same old, same old. Kind of on my own, right now."

I made a show of smiling my solitude off.

"We can't copulate any more, Tim."

But I hadn't been fishing! I looked, instinctively, at the boy, who, unperturbed, was spooning a chunk of mousse into his downturned face.

"Adalyn, I wasn't even hinting that..."

"You would probably like to, but it will no longer be necessary."

I stopped reaching for my cup.

"Necessary?"

At which point, as if on cue, the boy raised his head and I found myself staring at a photograph of myself aged six. A photo that had been retouched, given that 'my' eyes were a brighter emerald green, 'my' hair a darker, shinier brown, 'my' face neither solemn nor smiling, but placed in a neutral gear I was sure I'd never used. At least not when a child. I was unable to take my eyes off him:

"What's his name?"

"His name is Xylander."

I'd had a hunch it wouldn't be Timothy.

"Is he..."

I wished, then and there, I could have turned the latte into Armagnac.

"...ours?"

"In a way."

A shiver ran down my throat.

"In *what* way?"

"Are you doing anything special this afternoon?"

*

Her old model Kia was as quiet and bump-free as usual. She drove with mechanical precision, heading north-east with Xylander strapped into the back and me in the front passenger seat. When she got onto a dual carriageway, she pushed up the speed until it was doing well over what that car should have been capable of.

"Adalyn, once again, this car is performing like a Porsche."

Or had it been a Bentley? She glanced my way.

"Five years and three months ago, you asked me if I was a mechanic."

"And what did you say? I have trouble recalling conversations from half a decade back."

"I said, more or less."

"Right. But watch out for the radars, you don't want the police to pull you over."

"I am doing so."

And sure enough, she would occasionally decelerate and coast, then edge the vehicle back up to ninety miles per hour. Not that there was any device on the dash to warn her. I looked back at Xylander, who was staring out of the window.

Ours?

We slipped past Chelmsford, then Colchester.

"Where are we going, Adalyn?"

At Ipswich she turned gently onto the A14.

"You have been there before."

"I have?"

"A long time ago. It's possible that you don't remember."

She took a left onto the A12 and soon we were gliding past Martlesham, Woodbridge, Pettistree. The back of my mind started to mutter that I *had* been here before.

"I thought you would ask me more questions about Xylander."

"I don't know what to ask, Adalyn. You don't seem to want me to take on any responsibilities. But if you feel he needs a father…"

"No."

She slowed: another radar.

"We need to be impregnated three times. Mouth, vagina, anus."

I turned to her, wondering if she would let me out of the car if I asked her to stop.

"What are you saying now?"

"We," she paused, "need to be impregnated three times. Mouth -"

"I heard you the first time. What are you talking about?"

Her eyes shifted sideways to look at me, without her head following suit.

"Have you not guessed, Tim? Most people would have by now."

If she'd been hittable, I'd have cuffed her lightly on the shoulder.

"Just tell me, OK?" a note of anger in my almost shout, "Everything!"

Not that I was prepared to hear it. I looked at the tarmac as it slithered under the car.

"I'm not from here."

That much, I had surmised.

"So," I said, not really wanting a reply, "where *are* you from, Adalyn?"

"It doesn't matter. What matters, as far as you are concerned, is that *we* will not die so very young."

A bell jar placed itself over the car.

"Please tell me exactly what you mean. In language even a science correspondent can understand."

"You people normally live between fifty and eighty years and then you are gone, for good. As if you never existed."

A mile or so after Farnham, she turned onto a B road. We were heading seawards. Glimpses of countryside rang tinny chimes in my mind.

"It does not cross your minds to look to a future in which you will be different. In fact, it *cannot* cross your minds, any more than it can cross one of your cats' minds to learn how to read. We, on the other hand, value life, which is why we have sought ways of extending it."

That had actually occurred to us people. Perhaps she didn't know.

"Genetically?"

"More or less."

We passed through a place called Leiston. I was surprised to recognise the fish and chip shop.

"Through interbreeding. As our genitals are of a different nature, however, I thought it better that we interbred in the absence of light."

Her vaginal pumping of my penis came back to me so vividly it was as if I were inside her then and there. Now I knew why she hadn't wanted me to go down on her.

"All of us are interbred. We have no species. We choose those with whom we procreate once it has been ascertained that their genetic make-up will make it possible for our offspring to live longer even than we do. I will live for one hundred and ninety-three years. Xylander, for longer."

I felt as if my head were shrinking inside the silent car:

"You know what I think?"

"More or less."

I ignored that.

"I think you're making this up."

"You will see."

Aldringham. Darkness was moving in. The trees on either side of the road became sponges of bristle, outlined only when the headlights touched them.

"See what, Adalyn?"

"That you are always walking towards a closed door, you, your forebears, your offspring, just as you always have done and always will do. For you, life consists of nothing else but a path towards an exit that is locked..."

We shot past a sign that read Thorpeness.

"...We're almost there."

"I remember it now. Quite well."

"You were very young."

"Do you know how old?"

"Six."

She took a right along a lane, and drew up in front of a stand-alone cottage whose windows were boarded up, but which I recognised immediately as the place a friend of mine's parents and my own had rented for an Easter break. Thirty-four years ago. And I remembered that the friend, Ewan, was proud of being Scottish but spoke with a poshish English accent. And that we used to walk to where the North Sea lapped a thin stretch of beach, ice creams in our hands, sometimes. Other smithereens of childhood came to mind. My father kissing me on the crown of my head. His jokingly whipping out the whisky at midday before the politely disapproving grimaces of Ewan's Mum and Dad. His evening trips out to the pub, sometimes with Ewan's Dad, sometimes alone, because Ewan's Dad didn't want to go to the pub *every* night. My father waking me up when he got back by standing over my bed and saying 'you're a lovely little fellow' and stroking my forehead before leaving for the bedroom where my mother was already sleeping. My father, who never laid a finger on me.

Adalyn turned off the ignition and got out of the Kia. I followed her. There was a smell of wet leaves in the air. Swaying branches hissed. After a few seconds, Xylander got out as well. The stars were visible, showing off their distance. I hadn't stopped feeling the soft hand of my father or hearing his words soaked in love. Why had I rejected, despised, disclaimed him so much? Why – I asked myself as I stared involuntarily at the spark-flecked night – had I led my life, my one life, on the condition that it would not be like his? Was I – in the end – nothing more than the reverse side of his coin?

"Any time now."

Adalyn's measured voice.

"How did you know that I'd been here?"

"I saw you."

"Saw me?"

"Look up."

Suspended in perfect silence, lower than an aeroplane but way higher than the tallest of trees, was a disc, a row of modest lights along its side leading to one large dazzling one at its left tip.

Back then, the grown-ups had called, loudly, to me and Ewan and we had come outdoors and joined the grown-ups in staring at this object that was so visible and so still.

And I was six again, and at six time was timeless, time was something that happened to other people. Which is how I felt right now, as if thirty-four years had been flicked away: a child, cared for, loved, subject to paternal words of affection murmured in the dark. My eyes glued to the disc and its lights, I wondered how I could have forgotten I'd seen it before, but at six, I realised, words like 'alien' and 'otherworldly' meant nothing to me; and this object must have seemed to me to be just a bauble in the sky, pretty and a little boring, given that it wasn't doing anything much. But now, as I watched, it was precisely the alienness of it which transfixed me, its utter strangeness spelling out, yelling out, that I was of so very little consequence, and it struck me how wrong I'd been to think that my life and my ambitions were one and the same thing, when no ambitions would ever be fulfilled, no advancement would be of the kind I desired; that life, my own life, was nothing but something brief in which time would better be passed as pleasantly as possible because the end, for me – for all of us – would be solider than rock, realer than pain.

The disc hovered above me, a reminder of the shortness of my term. If Adalyn hadn't spoken, I might never have taken my eyes off it.

"It was from there that I saw you."

Of course she did. I heard myself saying:

"What now, Adalyn? What do I do?"

"I don't know. I just wanted," she raised a hand towards the craft, "to show you this."

I looked at it again, for what felt like a long time.

"Adalyn?"

She turned to me, her eyes barely visible.

"Yes?"

"Would you mind very much if we went back?"

Banyoles/Barcelona, 2020-2024

ACKNOWLEDGEMENTS

I would like to thank the Whitehead and MacAuslan families for having taken me with them on holiday to Thorpeness, Suffolk, back in 1970, where together we watched an unidentified flying object, identical to the one described at the end of this book.

Printed in Great Britain
by Amazon

37974714R00128